"I Don't Know How I Can Thank You."

He could think of a couple of ideas—and that was just for starters. The stupid part of his brain tried to argue that he just needed a woman. That was all. But he was starting to think he didn't need just any woman. He was starting to think he needed *this* woman.

"Let me take you to dinner—tonight."

Oh, yeah, he wanted her. But he wanted her to want him back. Just him. Not his money, not his band, not his financial skills and most certainly not his ability to keep the family together.

Her mouth parted, and she lifted her chin toward him. One kiss—what could it hurt? *Idiot,* he thought to himself as he moved closer. Like there was a shot in hell he could stop at just one.

Dear Reader,

Welcome to Crazy Horse Choppers, the family business run by the three Bolton brothers: Billy (the creative one), Ben (the numbers guy) and Bobby (the salesman). They live fast, ride hard and love fiercely.

Ben Bolton has long been the glue that holds his family—and company—together, but he's getting tired of putting his family and business first. The only thing Ben does for fun is play drums in a band. Even then, he has to keep the wheels from falling off. He can't even remember the last time he took a long ride to nowhere on his bike. Ben finds himself straddling a line between what he wants and what his family wants.

Then Josey White Plume walks into his office. She's looking for donations for a little school out on a Lakota reservation in South Dakota. Ben can't ignore the sparks that fly between them.

Josey also has to straddle a line—one between the white world she was raised in and the Lakota world of her ancestors. If she can get the school up and running, she will have earned her place in the tribe. A white man like Ben Bolton could jeopardize everything she's worked for.

Ben is faced with the question of his life—what's more important, his family or his own happiness?

Straddling the Line is a sexy story of finding one's place in the world. It's also my twist on cowboys and Indians: bikers and Indians! I hope you enjoy reading it as much as I enjoyed writing it. Be sure to stop by www.sarahmanderson.com and join me for the latest on Billy's and Bobby's stories!

Sarah M. Anderson

SARAH M. ANDERSON

STRADDLING THE LINE

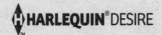

Recycling programs
for this product may
not exist in your area.

ISBN-13: 978-0-373-73245-6

STRADDLING THE LINE

Printed in U.S.A.

Books by Sarah M. Anderson

Harlequin Desire

A Man of His Word #2130
A Man of Privilege #2171
A Man of Distinction #2184
A Real Cowboy #2211
Straddling the Line #2232

*The Bolton Brothers

Other titles by this author available in ebook format.

SARAH M. ANDERSON

Award-winning author Sarah M. Anderson may live east of the Mississippi River, but her heart lies out West on the Great Plains. With a lifelong love of horses and two history teachers for parents, she had plenty of encouragement to learn everything she could about the Wild West.

When she started writing, it wasn't long before her characters found themselves out West. She loves to put people from two different worlds into new situations and see how their backgrounds and cultures take them someplace they never thought they'd go.

When not helping out at her son's elementary school or walking her rescue dogs, Sarah spends her days having conversations with imaginary cowboys and American Indians, all of which is surprisingly well tolerated by her wonderful husband. Readers can find out more about Sarah's love of cowboys and Indians at www.sarahmanderson.com.

To Hannah, the best middle sister I could have hoped for.

One

Josey took a deep breath, squared her shoulders and opened the door to Crazy Horse Choppers. She did this all while managing to completely ignore the impending sense of doom in her stomach—a sense of doom that told her soliciting educational donations from a motorcycle shop, no matter how upscale, was a hysterically bad idea.

The waiting room smelled of expensive leather and motor oil. Two black leather chairs with chrome accents sat on either side of a coffee table that was a sheet of round glass precariously perched on a collection of motorcycle handlebars twisted to form a base. Josey knew money when she saw it, and that furniture said custom-made. One wall was covered with autographed photos of her prey, Robert Bolton, with every kind of celebrity and pseudo-celebrity. A wall of glass separated the room from the actual shop. Several large, scary-looking men were working—with the kinds of tools she needed—on the other side of the wall. Bad idea or no, she was desperate. A shop class wasn't a class without shop tools.

That thought was cut short by a hard-looking woman—stringy hair that was supposed to be blond, tattoos practically coming out of her ears and more piercings than Josey could count—shouting, "Help you?" over thrashing music. Metallica, Josey thought.

The receptionist sat at a glossy black desk that looked to be granite. On the wall behind her hung a tasteful arrangement of black leather motorcycle jackets emblazoned with the Crazy Horse logo. The woman looked horribly out of place.

A second later, the music quieted—replaced with the high whine of shop tools cutting through metal. The receptionist winced. Josey immediately revised her opinion of the woman. If she had to listen to that whine all day, she'd resort to heavy metal to drown it out, too.

"Hello," Josey said, sticking out her hand. The woman looked at Josey's manicure and bangle bracelets and curled a lip. It was not a friendly gesture. Undaunted, Josey just smiled that much sweeter. "I'm Josette White Plume. I have a nine-thirty appointment with Robert Bolton." After another beat, Josey pulled her hand back. She kept her chin up, though.

So what if the receptionist looked like she'd come to work directly from an all-nighter? Bikers were people, too. At least that's what Josey was going to keep telling herself. A happy secretary was the difference between getting a purchase order pushed through in a week versus six months.

The receptionist—the name tag on her shirt said Cass—leaned over and flipped a switch on an intercom. "Your nine-thirty is here."

"My what?" The voice that came over the other end was tinny, but deep—and distracted.

Didn't Robert remember she was coming? She'd sent an email confirmation last night. The impending sense of doom grew. Josey swallowed, but managed to do so quietly.

Cass shot her a look that might be apologetic. "Your nine-thirty. More specifically, Bobby's nine-thirty. But he's in L.A.—or did you miss that?"

Wait—what? Who was in L.A.? Who was Cass talking to?

The doom in her stomach turned violent, hitting her with a wave of nausea. Dang, but she hated it when those stupid senses were on target.

She *thought* she'd been prepared. She'd spent weeks e-stalking Robert. She'd spent hours scrolling through his social networks, taking detailed notes on with whom he was meeting and why. She knew his favorite food (cheeseburgers from some dive in L.A.), where he bought his shirts (Diesel) and which actresses he'd been spotted kissing (too many to count). Her entire pitch—down to the close-cut, cap-sleeved, black wool banquette dress she was wearing—was built around the fact that Robert Bolton was a slick, ego-driven salesman who was making his family's choppers a national name. Heck, she knew more about Robert Bolton than she knew about her own father.

But none of that mattered right now. She was completely, totally unprepared. More than anything in this world, Josey hated being unprepared. Failure to plan was planning to fail. Being unprepared was about the same thing.

She'd been unprepared for Matt's rejection of her two years ago. She'd already been making plans, but in the end—because there was always an end—he'd chosen his family over her. She didn't "fit," Matt had claimed. And what he'd really meant was that, because she was a Lakota Indian, she didn't fit in his world. And, as a white man, he had no interest in fitting in hers. Not permanently.

The voice on the other end of the intercom grumbled, "I'm aware Bobby's in California. Is it a client or a supplier?"

"Neither."

"Then why the hell are you bothering me?" The intercom snapped off with an audible huff.

"Sorry," Cass said, clearly not. "Can't help you."

The dismissal—blunt and heartless—took all of her nerves and grated on them. Josey would not be ignored. If there was one thing she'd learned from her mother, it was that a silent Lakota Indian woman was a forgotten Lakota Indian woman. Because that's what she was—a Lakota woman.

She'd tried not being one, and that had just gotten her heart trampled on. After the affair with Matt had ended so spectacularly, she'd quit her job as a corporate fundraiser in New York and come home to her mother and her tribe. She'd somewhat foolishly thought they'd welcome her with open arms, but that hadn't happened, either.

So here she was, doing her best to prove that she was a full member of the tribe by building a school in the middle of the rez. But schools were expensive to build, more expensive to equip. So what if Crazy Horse Choppers had a reputation for being less than warm and fuzzy toward charitable causes? So what if Robert Bolton wasn't here? Someone was up there, and whoever it was would have to do. Screw being unprepared. Winging it had its advantages.

"Sure you can. You probably run this whole place, don't you?"

Cass smiled—without making eye contact, but it was still a smile. "Damn straight I do. Those boys would be lost without me."

Josey considered her line of attack. "You aren't old enough to have school-aged children—" Cass's head popped up, a pleased smirk on her face. She might be thirty-five or fifty-five—there was no telling with all those tattoos. But flattery could get a girl everywhere—if well done. And Josey could do it well. "I'm raising money for the vo-tech program at a new school, and I thought a chopper shop would be the perfect place to start."

So that was a lie. This was a last-ditch attempt to get some equipment. She'd started out approaching big manufacturers and had slowly worked her way down the food chain to local auto repair shops, remodeling contractors and even shop teachers at wealthier schools. Nothing. Not a damn thing.

Josey had gotten a twenty-two-year-old internet billionaire to give a few computers, a television chef who was on a healthy food kick to pay for some kitchen equipment and a furniture place to give her last year's model dining room tables and chairs to use for desks. She couldn't pry a band saw out of anyone's cold, dead hands. Against the vocal protests of a small group of school board members, led by Don Two Eagles, who wanted nothing to do with bikers in general and Boltons in particular, she'd decided to try Crazy Horse.

What did she have to lose? The school opened in five weeks.

"A school?" Doubt crept across Cass's face. "I dunno…"

"If I could just talk to someone…"

Cass shot her a mean look. Right. She was someone, so Josey pulled out a brochure and launched into her pitch.

"I represent the Pine Ridge Charter School. We're dedicated to the educational and emotional well-being of the underserved children of the Pine Ridge reservation—"

Cass held up her hands in surrender. "Okay, okay. I give." She flipped on the intercom again.

"Damn it, *what?*" On the bright side, the man on the other end was no longer distracted. However, he sounded mad. That sense of doom came rushing back in.

"She won't go."

"Who the hell are you talking about?" Excellent, Josey thought. Shouting.

Cass looked Josey up and down. There was something sneaky in her eyes as she said, "The nine-thirty. Says she's not going anywhere until she talks to someone."

He cursed. Rudely.

Whoa. F-bombs at nine-thirty in the morning. What on earth was she getting herself into?

"What is your problem, Cassie? You suddenly incapable of throwing someone out the door?" The shout was so loud that it briefly drowned out the sounds of the shop.

Cassie grinned like she was up for a round or two. She winked at Josey and said, "Why don't you come down here and throw her out yourself?"

"I do not have time for this. Get Billy to scare her off."

"Out on a test drive. With your father. It's all you today." She gave Josey a thumbs-up, as if this were a positive development.

The intercom made a God-awful screeching noise before it went dead. "Ben'll be right down," Cass said, enjoying being a pain in the backside. She pointed to a door in the wall of glass.

Maybe Josey should bail. Don Two Eagles had been right—Crazy Horse Choppers was a crazy idea. Josey put on her best smile as she thanked Cassie for helping out, hoping the smile would hide the panic hammering at her stomach.

Ben—Benjamin Bolton? Robert was the only member of the Bolton family who had joined the twenty-first century and had an online presence. Aside from a fuzzy group photo of the entire Crazy Horse staff and a generic-sounding history that traced how Bruce Bolton had founded the company forty years ago, she hadn't found anything usable about any other Bolton. She knew next to nothing about Ben. She thought he was the chief financial officer, and Robert's older brother. That was all she had to go on.

Before she'd made up her mind to stand her ground or take off, the glass door flew open. Ben Bolton filled the door frame, anger rolling off him in waves so palpable Josey fought to keep her balance. Should have run, she thought as Mr. Bolton roared, "What the hell—"

Then he caught sight of Josey. For a split second, he froze as he stared at her. Then everything about him changed. His jaw—solid enough to have been carved from granite—set as his eyes flashed with something that might have been anger, but Josey chose to interpret as desire.

Maybe that was just wishful thinking—in all likelihood, he was still angry—but without a doubt, Ben Bolton was the most handsome man she'd seen in a long time. Maybe ever. Heat flooded her cheeks, and she couldn't tell if that was attraction or just nerves.

He straightened up and puffed out his chest. Okay. This situation was salvageable. Brothers often liked the same things—music, games—why should women be any different? She didn't have enough time left to start over. She batted her eyelashes at him—a move she'd learned a long time ago worked despite being clichéd.

"Mr. Bolton? Josette White Plume," she said, advancing on him with a hand outstretched. His palm swallowed hers. He could have crushed her hand, but he didn't. His grip was firm without being dominating. She felt her cheeks get even warmer. "Thank you for taking the time to meet with me today." They both knew that he'd taken no such time, but a gentleman wouldn't contradict a lady. His reaction would tell her exactly what kind of man she was dealing with here. "I can't tell you how much I appreciate it."

Bolton's nostrils flared as the muscles along his jaw

tensed. "How can I help you, Ms. White…Plume?" He said her name like he was afraid of it.

Lovely. Hopefully he wouldn't start spouting all that PC nonsense about how she was an indigenous American of Native descent. As long as no one called her an Injun, the world could keep turning. She tightened her grip on his hand enough that one of his eyebrows notched up. She couldn't tell if his hair was black or brown in the dim light of the waiting room, but he'd look plenty good either way. "Perhaps we could discuss the particulars elsewhere?"

Suddenly, Bolton dropped her hand so fast that it bordered on pushing her away. "Why don't you come up to my office?" he asked, that flash of anger growing a little stronger.

Behind her, Cass snorted. Bolton shot her a look of pure warning, a look so hot Josey might have melted if it had been aimed square at her. But the dangerous look went right over her shoulder. By the time Ben Bolton turned those baby blues back to her, he was back to that no-man's-land between danger and desire. He stared down at her with an intensity she didn't normally encounter. He was waiting for her answer, she realized after a silent moment had passed. That was unusual. Most men just expected her to follow.

"That would be fine. I wouldn't want to keep Cass from her work."

Bolton narrowed those blue eyes in challenge, then turned on his heel and stalked out of the room. Josey barely had time to grab her briefcase before he'd disappeared out of sight.

"Good luck with that," Cass called out behind her in a cackling laugh.

In these shoes, Josey had to hurry to keep up with Bolton's long strides. He took the metal stairs two at a time, putting his bottom somewhere between hand and eye level. She shouldn't be openly gaping—not in public, anyway—but she couldn't help it. The whole back end was a sight to behold. Ben Bolton had wide shoulders packing the kind of muscle that a gray button-down shirt couldn't hide. His torso was long and lean, narrowing into a V-waist that was wrapped in a leather tool belt, which was way more cowboy than biker. His ankles were the safest place to look, Josey decided. Black denim jeans flowed over black cowboy boots with extra thick soles.

One thing was abundantly clear. Ben Bolton wasn't a normal CFO.

Below her, someone wolf-whistled. Before she could react—cringe, stick out her chin in defiance, anything—Bolton whipped his body to the railing and shouted, "That's enough!" in a voice powerful enough that Josey swore she could feel the vibrations through the metal stairs.

The sounds of the workshop—the clanging of hammers hitting metal, the whine of air compressors, a stream of words she could only vaguely discern as cursing—instantly died down to a low hum as Bolton bristled. For a moment, Josey thought she saw the railing bend in his grasp.

Josey's insides went a little gooey. This wasn't a *show* of power, this was *actual* power, so potent that she could nearly taste it. Ben Bolton commanded absolute respect, and he got it. She was an outsider here—she couldn't think of a time when she'd been more out of her league—but he still defended her without a second thought.

Bolton's glare swung down to where she stood precariously perched on a step, as if he thought she'd challenge the authority that had silently reined in twelve men armed with power tools. And then he was moving away from her, taking each step slowly and methodically this time.

Josey's pulse began to flutter at her wrists. She was used to men trying to impress her with their money, their things—all symbols of their power. This was a man who didn't appear to give a darn about impressing her. Heck, given the

way he now stood at the top of the stairs, arms crossed and
boot tapping with obvious impatience at her careful pace—
Josey was pretty sure he detested her. Somehow, that made
him that much more impressive.

When she neared the top, Bolton flung open a steel door
and waited for her to get her butt in the office with poorly dis-
guised contempt on his face. The doom ricocheting around
her belly grew harder to ignore. She'd missed her chance to
bolt, though. She had no choice but to tough this out.

The moment the door shut, the sounds of the shop died
away. Blissful silence filled her ears, but her eyes were now
taking the brunt of things. Bolton's office had so much metal
in it that Josey was immediately thankful the sun wasn't
shining in through the floor-to-wall windows. A stainless-
steel desk was underneath sprawling piles of papers. Filing
cabinets that matched the desk perfectly made up a whole
wall.

Everything in this gray office—down to the leather executive chair and the walls—said money. The leather-and-
chrome seats downstairs had said money, too. But this was
different. Downstairs screamed of someone dressing the
place to impress. Up here? Mr. Bolton didn't give a flying
rat's behind about impressing anyone. This was all about
control. Or Ben Bolton was color-blind. Either way, the
whole place looked depressingly industrial. In a wire mesh
trash can, she saw the remains of what had to be the recently departed intercom. Had he ripped it out of the wall?
Because of her?

No wonder Bolton was in a bad mood. If Josey had to
work in this office, she'd probably curl up into a lump of
iron ore and die.

Bolton motioned for her to sit in a shop chair—also
metal. He sat down and fixed her with another one of those
dangerous/desirous glares. He picked up a pen and began

bouncing the tip on the metal desk, which filled the air with a perfectly timed pinging. "What do you want?"

Oh, yeah, he was mad. Being as she had no plan B, Josey decided to stick with plan A. It was still a plan, after all. "Mr. Bolton—"

"Ben."

That was more like it. Familiarity bred success. "Ben," she started over. "Where did you go to school?"

Robert had graduated from a suburban high school in a wealthy area of Rapid City about twenty miles from where they sat. Odds were decent Ben had gone there, too.

"What?" Confusion. Also not bad. An opponent off-balance was easier to push in the right direction.

"I'd be willing to bet that you graduated near the top of your class, maybe played on the football team? You look like a former quarterback." Josey followed this up with one of her award-winning smiles—warm, full, with just a hint of flirting while she checked out those shoulders again. Wow. If Ben Bolton wasn't so intimidating, he'd be all kinds of hot. What did he look like without all the gray? Boy, she'd love to see what he looked like on a bike. He *had* to ride. He ran a motorcycle company.

Flattery usually got her everywhere—but not with this man. Ben's glare moved further away from desire and a heck of a lot closer to dangerous. "Valedictorian. And running back, All-State. So what?"

Josey managed to swallow without breaking her smile. The "All-State" was a good sign—bragging, if only just. But the pinging of the pen on metal got louder—and faster. Besides, she shouldn't be entertaining any sexual thoughts about another white man, not after the last debacle. She needed to stick to her goals here. Getting the school ready would earn her a place within the tribe—permanently.

"Your school had computers in every classroom, didn't

it?" Before he could demand "So what?" again, she kept going. "New textbooks every few years, top-of-the-line football helmets and teachers who actually understood what they taught, right?"

With a final, resounding clang, the pen stopped bouncing. Ben didn't stop glaring, though. Josey sat through the silence. She would not let this man know he intimidated her. So, chin up and shoulders back, she met his gaze and waited.

His hair was a deep brown, she realized. She could see the warm tones underneath—much browner than her own chestnut hair. A few streaks of salty white were trying to get a foothold at his temple, but his hair was cropped close in a no-nonsense buzz cut. The scowl he wore looked permanent.

Does he have any fun?

The question popped into her mind out of the blue, but it had nothing to do with game-planning her strategy. She found herself hoping he had *some* kind of fun, but she doubted it occurred within the walls of this steel box.

Finally, he broke the silence. "What do you want."

It wasn't a question—oh, no. A question would be getting off easy. This was an order, plain and simple.

That meant the answer to all of her previous questions was yes. She couldn't afford to waste any more time on setting up the pitch. If she didn't get on with it, he might take it upon himself to throw her out personally.

"Are you aware that the state of South Dakota has recently been forced to cut all funding to schools across the board?"

A look of disbelief stole over his face. "What?"

Right. He hadn't known she was coming; obviously, his brother hadn't told him about her. She pressed on. "As I told your brother Robert—"

"You mean Bobby."

She forced a smile at the interruption. Hot and intimidating sounded like a good combo, but the hotness just made the intimidating more intense. She prayed she wasn't about to start blushing. "Of course. As I told him, I'm seeking donations for the Pine Ridge Charter School." The look of disbelief got closer to incredulous, but Josey didn't give him a chance to interrupt her again. "Fewer than twenty percent of Lakota Sioux students graduate from high school—less than thirty percent go past the eighth grade." No, he didn't believe that, either, but then, few people did. The numbers were too unbelievable.

"Currently," she went on like a warrior out to count coup, "there is no school located within a two-hour drive from some parts of the reservation. Many students must be bussed two hours each way. If they're lucky, they get one of the good schools. If they're not, though, they get textbooks that are twenty years old, no computers, teachers who don't give a darn if their students live or die." The near-curse word got her something that might have been a quarter of a grin.

Maybe Ben liked things a little gritty. Well, Josey could do gritty. "Between the butt-numbing trip on buses that break down all the time, the crappy education and the unrelenting bullying for being American Indians, most choose to drop out. People expect them to fail. Unemployment on the reservation is also near eighty percent. Any idiot can see that figure mirrors the dropout rate almost precisely." She batted her eyes again. "You don't look like an idiot to me."

The pinging started back up. The only thing he was missing was a cymbal. "What do you want?" His words were more cautious this time.

He was listening. Suddenly, Josey had a good feeling about this. Ben Bolton was a numbers guy—he liked his facts hard and fast. But he was a biker, too—so he could appreciate things that were rougher, tougher and just a little bit dirty.

Her face—and other parts—flushed hot. So much for not blushing.

His eyes widened, the blue getting bluer as he noticed her unprofessional redness. The corner of his mouth crooked up again as he leaned a few inches toward her. A small movement, to be sure—but she felt the heat arc between them. Desire kicked the temperature up several notches.

Wow. One slightly unprofessional thought, and she was on the verge of melting in the middle of a pitch. This wasn't like her. She prided herself on keeping business and pleasure separate. Some people thought they could buy her with the right donations, but Josey never even allowed that kind of quid pro quo to enter the conversation.

With everything she had, Josey pushed on. She had a job to do. Pleasure came later—if it came at all. She needed to get the school ready more than she needed what would no doubt be a short-lived fling. She didn't have time for flings, especially with a white man.

She handed Ben the three-color brochure she'd designed herself. "The Pine Ridge Charter School is designed to give our Lakota children a solid foundation, not only for their education, but for their lives. Studies have shown that graduating from high school raises a person's total lifetime earnings over a million dollars more than a dropout. All it takes is a fraction of that cost up-front."

He flipped her brochure over. She could see him processing the photos she'd taken of the happy kids crowded around her mother for a story at a family gathering, and the architectural drawings for the six-room schoolhouse that was only half built out on the flat grassland of the rez. "*Your* children?" His eyes cut down to her bare left hand.

"I am a registered member of the Pine Ridge tribe of the Lakota Sioux." She hated having to add the "registered" part, but there it was. The red in her hair made people look at her like she was just a wannabe. She had her grandfather to thank for her hair, but that was the only part of him that showed up. "My mother will be the principal and chief educator at the new school. She has a doctorate in education and has spent a lifetime teaching *our* children how important a good education is to them—and to the tribe."

"Which explains why you sound like you graduated from high school."

Now it was her turn to glare. "My MBA is from Columbia. Yours?"

"Berkley." He flipped the brochure onto his desk. "How much?"

"We aren't begging for money." Mostly because she knew she wouldn't get it, but it was also a point of pride. The Lakota didn't beg. They asked nicely. "We're offering a unique sponsorship opportunity for businesses around the state. In return for supplies, we will provide free publicity in several forms. Our website will have a detailed list of contributors on our site, as well as links and feedback to your own internet presence." She leaned forward and tapped her finger on the web address at the bottom of the brochure. When she looked up at Ben again, his eyes were fastened on her face—not her cleavage. But the intensity of his gaze made her feel like he was looking down her dress.

Slowly, she sat back in her seat. His eyes never budged, but the inherent danger that had lurked in them since word one was almost gone. Nothing but desire was left. "Everything donated to the school will be labeled with the sponsors' information, helping your business build brand-loyal customers while equipping them with the tools they need to be able to afford your products—"

"You're going to put ads in the school?"

No, Ben Bolton was nobody's idiot. "I prefer not to think

of them as ads—sponsorship. More along the lines of a pizza parlor sponsoring a T-ball team."

His shoulders moved, a small motion that might have been a sign of laughter. "So, ads."

"For your business," she added, undeterred. "Crazy Horse Choppers has been around for forty years, and given how you built this state-of-the-art production facility a few years ago, I have every reason to believe you'll be around for another forty."

He tilted his head in her direction, a sign of respect from a man who commanded it. So she wasn't completely unprepared—a comforting thought. His appreciation was short-lived. "I'm only going to ask this one more time. What do you want?"

"The Pine Ridge Charter School is designed to provide children with not only a world-class education—" he began to ping the pen on the desktop again "—but job training. To that end, we are asking for the equipment necessary to launch an in-depth vocational technology program."

A smile—a real one, the kind of smile that made a woman melt in her business dress—graced his face. Whoa. *All* kinds of hot. "Finally. The point. You want me to give you shop tools for free."

The way he said it hit her funny. A note of panic started growing again in her belly. "In so many words, yes."

He picked up the brochure again. He looked like he was really weighing her proposal, but then he said, "No." He set the brochure carefully to one side and put both hands on the desk, palms-down. For all the world, he looked like he was about to vault the darn thing. "Look. You're obviously intelligent and obviously beautiful. But this business operates on razor-thin margins. I'm not about to give away a bunch of tools for nothing."

A small, girly part of her went all gooey. He thought she

was beautiful. *Obviously* beautiful. "Not even for the free advertising?" Her voice came out pinched. She couldn't manage to keep the defeat out of it.

His shoulders flexed. "Not even for the free advertising."

He was staring at her again, waiting to see if she'd challenge him. She swallowed and bit her lower lip. The barest glimmer of desire crossed his face.

"Isn't there…anything I can do to change your mind?" The moment the words left her mouth, she wished she could take them back. She didn't make offers like that, ever. So why the heck had she just said that?

Not that it worked. She thought she saw his pupils dilate, but it was hard to be sure because his eyes narrowed to angry slits. "Does that work?"

No, she wanted to tell him, because she'd never made the offer before. Yes, he was hot. He was also arrogant, domineering and quite possibly heartless—a real Scrooge in leather. All reasons her mouth should have stayed firmly closed. It didn't matter whether or not Ben Bolton was good in bed. Or on his desk. Or even on one of his choppers, for that matter. It didn't matter if she wanted to find out—or it *shouldn't* matter. But with one mistaken sentence, suddenly it did.

And he wouldn't even say yes to that.

The rejection stung her pride, and she wanted to tell him to go to hell, but she never got the chance. At that moment, a huge crash reverberated up through the floor of his office, loud enough that every piece of metal in the joint shook with enough force that she had to grab on to her chair to keep from falling off it.

Ben slumped forward, weariness on his face. He held up one hand and did a silent countdown—three, two, one— before his phone buzzed.

"What?" He didn't sound surprised.

The voice on the other end was loud enough that even Josey winced. Ben had to hold the receiver a half a foot away from his head.

"I'm busy" was all he said, slamming the phone down. "Miss White Plume..." He paused, as if he was waiting for her to reciprocate his "Ben" with her "Josey." When she didn't, he went on with an apologetic shrug. "I'd recommend coming over here," he said, motioning to his side of the desk. Another huge crash shook the floor. "Right *now*."

Closer to him—mere seconds after that rejection? The next crash seemed closer—like a herd of buffalo were stampeding up the stairs. Josey was in no mood to be trampled. She gathered her things and scurried over to Ben's side of the desk. He took a protective step in front of her just as the door was thrown open with enough force that she was sure she saw the hinges come loose.

A man—no, more like a monster—burst into the room. He was huge—easily six-five, with a long handlebar mustache that was jet-black. His muscles were barely contained by a straining blue T-shirt, which matched the do-rag he had tied over his head. His eyes were hidden by wraparound shades, making it impossible to know how old he was. "Goddamn it," he roared, the noise echoing off all the metal, "you tell that bastard you call a brother that I told him to—"

Josey's presence registered, and the man bit off his curse at the same time an even bigger man, covered with enough facial hair to render him indistinguishable from a black bear, shoved into the room. "I told you, there's no way you can pull off that asinine idea, and—"

The man with the handlebar mustache punched the bear in the shoulder and jerked a thumb toward Josey. She couldn't help it. Even though she was mad as all get-out at Ben for turning her down—both times—she found herself cowering behind him. Compared to the wall of bikers hollering on the other side of the desk, Ben was the safest thing in the room. He leaned in front of her a little more and put one hand behind him, keeping her contained. She was furious with him, more furious with herself—but that simple act of protection left her feeling grateful.

"Aw, hell," the bear muttered.

"What you got there, son?"

Ah. So the man with the handlebar mustache was Bruce Bolton, chief executive officer of Crazy Horse Choppers—and father of the Bolton men. Which meant that the bear behind him was probably Billy, the creative force behind Crazy Horse. Looked like that test drive they'd been on hadn't gone well.

Josey didn't particularly like the way the senior Bolton was eyeing her—and she especially didn't like being a "what." Not that she could be sure—he still had on his sunglasses—but she got the distinct feeling he was undressing her with his eyes.

Ben's shoulders flexed. "I told you, I'm busy." He reached over and picked up his phone. His motions seemed calm, but she could sense the coiled tension just below the surface.

The worst place in the world had to be the middle of a Bolton brawl, because it sure looked like all three of them were ready to throw down, here and now. Maybe that's why the whole office was done in metal. Easier to wash off the blood.

"Cassie, please escort our guest to her car," he said, icy daggers coming off his words. He set the phone back down, positioning his body just a fraction more between Josey and his father.

No one moved; no one said a thing. She'd been scared before, sure. She'd talked her way out of being felt up by associates of her grandfather; she'd beaten the living crap out of a boy who'd thought she was an easy target back in high school. But this? Hands down, the scariest situation she'd ever gotten herself into.

Cass appeared, shoving her way into the room. "Damn, Bruce, you're scaring her," she said, hip-checking the older man out of the way. "Come on," she said to Josey. "Let them fight it out in private."

Ben nodded, a small movement that she took to mean she was safe with the only other woman in the place. Moving slowly, she stepped around the desk, careful to avoid the older man. The younger one gave her plenty of room before he favored her with a familiar-looking nod that bordered on a polite bow.

"Miss White Plume," Ben called to her as soon as she was clear of his office's threshold. "Good luck."

Cass shut the door, which wasn't enough to block the sound of a battle royal erupting behind it. Josey didn't get the chance to wish him the same.

She had the feeling she'd just about used up all of her luck for the day.

Two

Stick's chord from "Dirty Deed Done Dirt Cheap" still hung in the air as Ben attacked his drums with a wild energy for the next song. Van Halen's "Hot for Teacher" was his best song, one he could literally beat the hell out of.

The groupies crowded around the front of the stage at The Horny Toad Bar screamed as Ben tore through his big solo. Stick, his oldest friend in the world, came in hard on the guitar riff, and—in that brief moment before Rex started singing—Ben could pretend that the Rapid City Rollers were a real rock band, not a weekend cover band.

Try his best, though, Rex couldn't come close to David Lee Roth—or Sammy Hagar, for that matter—so the illusion that Ben was a professional drummer never lasted. Sure, they were popular here, but South Dakota didn't have a lot of people in it. Still, this was Ben's song, and he gave it his all. The crowd was on its feet, somewhere between dancing and moshing in drunken delight.

Saturday nights were the best. For one long night once a week, Ben wasn't a CFO. He didn't have to worry about Billy's slow production pace costing the company too much money. He didn't care if the banks floated him the stop-gap loans he needed. He could forget about whatever Bobby was screwing around with. And most of all, he didn't even have to think about his father, who was determined to grind the family business into the ground just to prove that his way was not only better than Ben's way, but that his way was the only way. For one night a week, Ben didn't have to care about how Dad looked at him with nothing but disappointment in his eyes. None of that mattered. On Saturday nights, Ben was a drummer. That was all.

He loved having something he could beat the hell out of, over and over, but instead of leaving destruction in his wake like Dad did, he made something that he loved—something beautiful, in its own brutal way. Something that other people loved, too. It wasn't the same as Billy's bikes, but it was Ben's and Ben's alone. A week's worth of frustration went into each beat.

Something was different tonight. Rex was hitting most of the high notes, and the crowd was eating it up. The Horny Toad was one of their best gigs—they played here once a month. Ben should be enjoying himself. But no matter how hard he hit his drums, he couldn't get the sound of one Josette White Plume saying, "Isn't there…anything I can do to change your mind?" out of his head.

That voice had been floating around in his dreams for eight freaking days now, and he was damn tired of it. It had gotten to the point where he'd begun to think he should have taken her up on her offer—get her out of his system before she'd gotten into it.

The hell of it was that he couldn't quite nail down *why* he was stuck on her. Sure, she'd been beautiful—but the

Horny Toad was loaded with hot chicks tonight. Yeah, she was probably the smartest woman he'd talked to in weeks—months, even. And, okay, he'd have to admit that her fiery, take-no-prisoners business pitch combined with that note of vulnerability at the end, right before his family had crashed the joint, had made his body throb.

But she was just a woman. Maybe that was it, he thought as he wailed away on his drums. Maybe it had just been too long since he'd had a woman. Hell.

Stick held the high note at the end for an extra beat while Ben let the cymbals have it at the end. Their eyes met and they nodded in time, cutting off at the same moment. The crowd howled for more, which was a nice feeling. Someone threw a bra onto the stage, which Toadie, the bassist, snatched up and waved in victory. "We'll be back after a little meet 'n' greet break," Rex announced, tossing his guitar pick to an unnaturally busty blonde.

"You coming?" Stick asked as the house music filled the bar. Rex and Toadie had already been enveloped by the groupies, and Ben knew Stick was itching to get out there and join them.

Ben didn't go anymore, but Stick always asked. He was a good friend. "No," he started to say, but then a woman caught his eye.

She was tall and lean and wearing a white sequined tank top over a nice chest that caught some of the stage lights and made her glow, even though he was wearing sunglasses in a dimly lit bar. But that wasn't what drew his attention. No, something about the way she was looking at him…

No. It couldn't be. Could it?

The woman turned to talk to someone else, but then glanced back over her shoulder at him. Cascades of dark hair spilled down her back, coming to an end just above the kind of ass that *would* haunt a man. He'd caught just a glimpse of her walking out of his office before Dad and Billy had erupted into World War III, but he wasn't likely to forget it anytime soon.

No doubt about it. Josette White Plume was in the house.

"Yeah," he told Stick, "I think I will." Together, they hopped off the side of the stage and ducked around the chicken wire.

Someone grabbed his butt, and a few chicks tried to throw themselves in front of him, but Ben ignored them all. He was focused on the woman in the sequined top.

Maybe he was wrong, he thought as he got closer. Her back was still to him, and all that hair was throwing him off. The woman who'd come to his office had had a twist pinned up in a classy, elegant style that matched her classy, sleek dress. The woman a few feet away from him wore skintight jeans and had long hair that hung in loose curls. He couldn't tell about the color in this light, but he was sure he'd recognize that reddish black anywhere.

He closed the remaining distance, grabbed the woman's bare arm and spun her around. She tried to jerk away with such force that it pulled him into her. His sunglasses came off in the resulting jostling.

"Hey!" A smaller woman—clearly Native American—pushed her way between Ben and his prey. "Get your hands off her, you creep!"

Now that he had her face-to-face, without his sunglasses, he could see the red in her hair—and the fire in her eyes. "What the— Oh!" Recognition set in, and the anger became shock. "Ben?"

Ben glanced down at his hand and was surprised to see that he was still holding her. Her skin was creamy smooth against his. In her other hand, she held a bottle. "What are you doing here?"

"Who's asking?" the smaller woman demanded. She sounded comfortable being the boss.

"No, Jenny—let me explain."

"What's to explain?" The woman named Jenny shoved Ben's chest. "He can't just grab you, Josey."

Josey. God, what a pretty name. Would he ever get this woman out of his head?

Josette—Josey—blushed. "Jenny, this is Ben Bolton, CFO of Crazy Horse Choppers."

"Wait—you're the guy who didn't give us anything?" She sniffed in distaste. Ben decided he kind of liked Jenny. She had spunk.

But Josey—Josey had fire. The heat coming off that woman was making him sweat with need. "Jenny! Ben," she went on, hell-bent on formal introductions in the middle of one of the grimier bars in the state, "this is Jenny Wahwasuck. She's one of the teachers at our new school."

"And her cousin, so you just watch yourself, buddy." Jenny crossed her arms and glared at him.

Someone bumped him from behind, shoving him into Josey. Jenny made loud noises of protest.

Screw this. He couldn't find out what she was doing here in the middle of the bar with her cousin watching him like a hawk. He leaned in close to whisper, "I need to talk to you—alone," in Josey's ear—which was a mistake. Up close, he could smell her scent, something light and clean, with a hint of citrus. She smelled delicious.

It took all of his willpower to lean back, but he didn't get far. Instead, he found himself staring into her big brown eyes. The slick, overconfident ballbuster who'd talked her way into his office was gone, and in her place was someone who looked surprisingly sweet and vulnerable—considering the bar they were in.

She nodded and turned to her cousin. "I'll be right back, okay?"

"Wait—what? No way!" Jenny tried to shove Ben back, but he didn't give her any leeway this time.

"It's about the school," Josey said.

Except it wasn't. But if that was the lie that worked, he was willing to nod and play along. Jenny rolled her eyes in frustration, but turned to Ben and said, "If she's not back here in one piece in ten minutes…"

"I just want to talk to her."

The hell he did. He wanted to do everything *but* talk, a fact made all the more clear when Josey slipped her hand into his and waited for him to lead her away.

Ben plowed through the crowd like a bulldozer. There was only one place quiet enough to *not* have a conversation in this joint—the small closet that served as the band's dressing room.

As he worked his way back there, two conflicting emotions ran headlong into each other. First off, he was pissed. Saturday night was his night off. He didn't have to think about people taking and taking and taking from him until he had nothing left to give, about how he never got anything back. He didn't want to think about some school in the middle of nowhere, and he sure as hell didn't want to have to think about the bottom line.

The other thing barreling through his thoughts was the way Josey had laced her fingers with his, the way his thumb was stroking small circles around her palm and the way he wanted to bury his face in her hair and find out if she tasted of oranges or limes.

He pulled her into the dressing room with more force than he needed—she came willingly—and slammed the door shut. *Don't touch her,* he told himself, because touching her again would be a mistake, and Ben wasn't the kind of guy who made mistakes. He was the kind of guy who fixed other people's mistakes.

Still, that didn't explain why she was backed against the wall, trapped between his arms. Hey, at least he wasn't touching her.

"Why are you here?" he demanded, keeping his voice low. No need to shout, not when he was less than a foot from her face.

She licked her lips. They were a deep plum color, like a fine wine begging to be savored.

Not. Touching. Her.

"Jenny's son is at her mother's house. It's a girl's night out...." Her voice trailed off as she looked at him through thick lashes.

He was not going to fall for that old trick—no matter how well it was working. "You told her we were going to talk about the school. I already said no. How did you track me down?"

"I came to hear the band." Her voice had dropped to a feather whisper. He couldn't help it if he had to lean in closer to hear it. "I came for the music."

"Bull." No way did he believe that—not even if he really wanted to.

She swallowed, then one hand reached up and traced his cheek. *He* wasn't touching her, but the mistake was huge nonetheless. Heat poured into him, all coming from that one, single touch.

Just a woman, he told himself. He just needed a woman, and she fit the bill. That didn't explain why he couldn't look at her and feel her at the same time without doing something he knew he'd regret, so he shut his eyes. It didn't block out the sound of her voice, though.

"I've seen you play before."

"Prove it."

"Fat Louie's—late last March, although I forget the day. The singer was different that night." Her other hand palmed his other cheek. So soft. So sweet. "Not quite as good as this guy, but not bad."

Bobby had taken the mic that night—Rex had the flu. She wouldn't know that unless she was telling the truth… but Bobby had left with a smokin' hot woman that night, and raved about the sex for weeks after that. "Are you some kind of groupie? Did you go home with him?"

"I'm a corporate fundraiser." Her voice packed more heat this time, taking his challenge head-on. "I don't do one-night stands, and I don't screw men I don't know."

His body throbbed. Two tense meetings—did this qualify as knowing each other? Was screwing on the table? Damn. It *had* been too long since he'd had a woman.

"Before that, it was at Bob's Roadhouse," she went on. "I think that one was right before Thanksgiving. You did a metal version of 'Over the River.'" Her thumbs traced his cheeks. Yeah, he remembered doing that. Rex hadn't stopped with the stupid "stuffing the turkey" jokes all night long.

He felt his head dip, although he had no idea if she was pulling him or if he was doing it himself.

"And before that—"

He kissed her before he could stop himself. His tongue hit her lips, and she opened for him. Lemons. She tasted like lemonade, sweet and tart and just right. She made a small mewing sound in his mouth, a sound of surrender.

Somehow, he managed to break away from her. He had to, before he did something vulgar like have sex with a woman he barely knew in a closet in a bar.

"I didn't know." Her voice shook this time. "I should have guessed—the way you drummed the desk with that pen— but I didn't recognize you. You always wear the sunglasses and the bandanna…. I didn't know it was you."

He kissed her again, rougher this time. His teeth nipped at her lower lip before his tongue tangled with hers. He shouldn't believe her, but he wanted to, more than he'd wanted anything else. He wanted to believe that this beautiful, intelligent woman liked his music without wanting anything else from him. That she might like him without wanting shop equipment or school supplies or anything.

She wrapped her arms around his neck and pulled him to her. He felt her stiff nipples press against his chest, felt the heat when she tilted her hips up into his. God, she really wanted him, as much as he wanted her.

He wanted to believe her.

But he couldn't.

He shoved himself away with everything he had. He sucked in air—which didn't help, because her scent hung around him. Her chest—in all its glory—was heaving, a sight he'd love to behold any other day. He swiped his hand across his mouth in a desperate attempt to erase her sweetness. Mistake. He'd made a mistake, but he couldn't tell who he was madder with—her, or himself. "Does that work?" he demanded.

"Does what work?" She had the damn nerve to look innocent and confused.

"That—using sex to trap me." And he'd fallen right into it. Damn it, skin-to-skin contact was a major mistake. "Does that get you what you want?"

He braced himself for the crack across the face—he expected nothing less than outright condemnation and denial from her—but she didn't smack him. Instead, a look of pain crossed her face for a second before it disappeared underneath something else. Something sad, which made him feel like the world's biggest jerk. "You already said no—I wasn't—"

Her eyes skimmed over his arms—and found his tats.

Damn sleeveless T-shirts, he cursed silently. She could see the one that had Mom's birth—and death—date. He thought about turning the other way, but that would be worse, because then she'd see the one for Moose, his dog. He crossed his arms and gave her his meanest stare. She didn't even blink.

For a blinding second, he hated her—the way she seemed to look right into him, the way she made him feel like hell for being a jerk, the way she had the nerve to feel bad for him—he hated all of it.

When the hell would this break end? If he didn't start beating his drums again right now, he was going to have to punch a wall or something.

Then she did something even weirder. She came to him, touched his tats and whispered, "I'm sorry." And then she kissed him. After he'd all but called her a slut to her face, she kissed him—again.

This was different—softer, easier. Against his will, his arms uncrossed and then folded again, with her inside them. Her weight was warm and comfortable against his chest. She fit well there.

Something strange happened. The solitary quiet he usually felt when he thought about Mom seemed less solitary. It almost seemed like Josey White Plume understood how alone he felt surrounded by his brothers, how hard it was to always have to be the responsible one, how exhausting the daily battle with his father was, how damn *tired* he was of not being good enough. She understood it all and was happy to take some of the burden off his shoulders.

She broke the kiss and rested her forehead against him. Oddly, that was almost as good as the kiss. Forget the last time he'd gotten laid. When was the last time he'd held a woman—without feeling like she wanted something from him?

Josey's chest rose and fell against his, strong and steady.

Her arms were around his neck, holding their bodies together. For some stupid reason that should have everything to do with his groin but didn't, Ben would have been happy to stand here and hold her all night long.

He didn't get the chance. Right then, someone began to pound on the door.

"Benny! Zip it up, kick the chick out and let's rock!"

Josey jolted, and Ben was forced to let her go. She straightened her top, shook her hair out and licked her lips. Could she still taste him, like he could taste her?

"I came for the music," she said, her voice reaching his ears over the pounding on the door. "No strings attached."

"No strings attached," he agreed. So why did it feel like she'd just bound part of her to part of him?

The band continued banging on the door like it was a secondhand drum set. He didn't need his spine rearranged, so he got out of the way.

Toadie, Stick and Rex fell into the room. Rex was giggling— a sure sign that he was happily on his way to roaring drunk. When they caught sight of Josey, the merry band of idiots came to a screeching halt. Toadie was the first to make his move. "Holding out on us, Benny? Or were you planning on sharing?"

Ben's thoughts went in two directions. One part of him wondered how many shots they had done and if they would be able to get through the next set before Rex passed out on the floor.

The other part of him got real pissed, real fast. He wasn't about to let these jerk-offs call her character into question— never mind that he'd just done the very same thing. Whether she was conniving or innocent, Josey White Plume was no floozy, happy to let any slimeball do shots off her boobs. He'd be damned if he let these morons drool all over her. She deserved better than that.

Rex punched Toadie in the arm and stepped up. "Ma'am,

ignore the cretin," he said, doffing an imaginary hat and mis-pronouncing *cretin*. "And, if I may be so bold, may I suggest joining me after the show's over? You are clearly way, *way* out of Benny's league. Stick with me, and I'll show you what a real man can do."

The next thing Ben knew, he was shoving Rex, and Rex was shoving back. Stick tried to grab Ben, and Toadie made a halfhearted effort to hold Rex, but Ben didn't care. Rex wanted a fight? Fine. Ben would enjoy beating the living hell out of him.

He didn't have to. Instead of ducking for cover, Josey stepped between him and Rex. She looked the singer up and down, shaking her head with distaste. She turned back to him and smiled—whoa. How could a woman look so fiery and so innocent at the same time?

"Thanks for the offer, but I prefer drummers."

So hot, he thought as she stood on her tiptoes and brushed her lips over his. The guys began catcalling behind them, but Ben didn't give a damn. He just wanted to remember this moment, this feeling of no strings attached.

She started to pull away, but he grabbed her around the waist. "I'll find you after the show."

"Are you guys going on or what?" The bar's manager stuck his peevish head through the door. "It's getting ugly out here."

With the door open, Ben could hear the riot about to break out in the bar. Josey slipped from his arms and finally he got to appreciate the sight of Josey White Plume walking away.

Rex looked like he was going to pop an O-ring laughing. "Not a word," Ben said, cracking the knuckles on each hand with his thumb—a trick he'd learned from Dad, one that was pretty effective when a guy was trying to look menacing. "Not one stinking word."

Toadie made the motion to lock his mouth and throw

away the key, but Rex still looked like he wanted to go a round or two.

"Get on the damn stage!" the manager shouted over the shattering sound of glass.

Right. That's what they were here for—the music. The only thing that had never let Ben down and never demanded something he couldn't give.

Through the rest of the next set, he kept searching the crowd for Josey. The feeling of her lips against his stayed with him, song after song. He caught sight of her a few times—the sequins on her shirt gave her a glow that stood out in the smoky bar—but then the crowd would shift and he'd lose her again.

Rex split as soon as the gig was up; Toadie took his amp and bailed, too. Normally, Ben was in charge of getting their equipment out of the bar in one piece. Not tonight. He shot Stick a look and headed out to find Josey. No-strings-attached sex could be amazing sex, and maybe if he had some amazing sex, he'd be able to get her out of his head.

She wasn't in the bar; no sign of her in the parking lot. He even had a waitress check the bathroom—nothing.

Gone.

Where the hell did she go?

Josey rested her head on the steering wheel, waiting for her mind to clear. The intersection was empty at this ungodly hour of the morning, so she was able to think without being honked at. Thankfully, Jenny had cut out early—something about midnight being past her bedtime—so Josey could think without being judged.

Which way should she go?

If she went right, she'd be within the city limits of Rapid City inside of ten minutes. Another fifteen until she got to the gentrifying, hip downtown neighborhood where her apartment was above an upscale children's boutique. It was a nice place—a small studio, but one where the heat and plumbing always worked and she could watch TV while surfing the internet. All the conveniences of modern life—conveniences she'd become accustomed to while going to school out East and living as a mostly white woman—were at her fingertips when she was at her apartment.

If she turned right, she'd sleep late, grab a cappuccino and a croissant from the Apollo Coffee Co. down the street and do some work. She'd send a few follow-up emails to sponsors, do a little research into other possible donors.

If she turned right, things would be quiet. Calm.

Lonely.

If she went left, though, she'd get onto Highway 90. In five minutes, Rapid City would be nothing but a glow in her rearview mirror. In twenty minutes, she'd hit the edge of the rez, and in forty-five minutes, she'd be at her mom's double-wide trailer. She'd try to be quiet when she got in, but Mom would wake up anyway. She'd say, "Oh, Josey, I'm glad you're home," the same thing she said every single time Josey came over. It didn't matter if she was visiting for lunch, staying for the weekend or just showing up, Mom was always glad she was home. Then Mom would touch the picture of Dad she kept on top of the TV and shuffle back to bed.

If Josey turned left, she'd make her own tea in the morning and eat a knockoff brand of cereal for breakfast. She'd spend the next several days working on the school. Her back would try to kill her, her manicure would be shot to heck and she'd be face-to-face with the unavoidable fact that the school—the legacy her grandfather left her to complete—would not be ready for the grand opening and some members of the tribe would hold that against her. Things would be crazy. Messy. Unfinished.

Just like things with Ben were unfinished. If she turned

around, she'd be back at the bar in less than five minutes. She could find Ben, pick up where she'd left off—God help her, she had no idea a man could kiss like that—and then…

No. She couldn't go back. She'd done the correct thing, leaving the bar before the last set had ended. Correct, because Ben Bolton wasn't arrogant, domineering and heartless like she'd first thought. Well, maybe he was all of those things, but underneath that, there was more to him—something lost, something lonely. Something that didn't fit, no matter how hard he tried. That was the something Josey recognized.

Ben Bolton was a dangerous man because he was someone she could *care* for.

She couldn't let herself get involved with him. It didn't matter how good the kiss had been. The last time she'd followed her heart instead of her head, she'd gotten it trampled into small, unrecognizable bits. Plus, a lot of people on the rez didn't look kindly upon interracial dating. She'd worked so hard for so long, trying to prove her bona fides to the tribe. No white man, not even Ben Bolton, was worth risking that kind of pain.

A horn honked behind her, startling her out of her thoughts.

Left or right?

The horn blared, the driver's impatience obvious.

Josey turned left.

Three

Ben took a deep breath. He hated this quarterly meeting with his father. Actually, it was the quarterly report from the chief financial officer to the chief executive officer, but Ben could never shake the feeling that he was in sixth grade, marching to his doom to explain the two Cs he'd gotten. Despite the fact that Ben had graduated as the valedictorian, Dad had always held those two Cs against him. Hell, he wouldn't be surprised if the old man threw them back in his face today.

Ben was getting ahead of himself. Maybe this would go well.

And pigs might sprout wings, he thought as he knocked. The sooner he got this over with, the sooner he could go back to running the business.

"Dad?"

"Come in."

Ben swung the door open and, just like he did every time

he went into Dad's office, he grimaced at the piles of paper that covered every available surface. Although it hadn't been an official reason for moving to the new building, Ben had hoped that relocating would help Dad pare down the pit of paperwork.

It hadn't. Bruce Bolton was the kind of old school that believed "if it ain't broke, don't fix it" was a battle cry in the war against technology. Bobby had gotten Dad on a computer and set up email, but the old man still insisted on printing out every single piece of electronic communication and then "filing" it according to a system that no one but he understood. Hell, the last time Ben had ordered a new printer, Dad had ranted about how that old dot-matrix printer that fed the green-and-white-striped paper on reels was the best piece of technology he'd ever owned. That printer had been a dinosaur twenty years ago—just like Dad.

But facts were facts, and the facts were, Crazy Horse Choppers was still Bruce Bolton's business. Sure, Billy made the bikes, Ben balanced the books, and Bobby...well, he did something. Bruce was still the sole owner, and he still insisted on approving every single expenditure. Hence the quarterly meeting, where Ben tried to beat some sense into Dad's head and Dad's head only got harder.

"Quarterly report," Ben said, trying to find a place on Dad's desk where he could set the file. He'd given up on emailing the report a long time ago.

"Still in the black?" That was all Dad cared about. His world was black and white—or, more specifically, black and red. He didn't care about what it took to keep those numbers in the black, and he didn't even care how much black there was. He only cared that the bottom-line number was black. It seemed to Ben that Dad set a pretty low bar for success.

"Yes, still in the black. We shipped thirty-seven units, took in orders for forty-five bikes and have our delays down to twenty-eight days." Of course, Ben had had to get several loans to bridge the gap between delivery and payment, but those facts bored Dad.

This was no way to run a business in today's world. If Ben could get Dad to sign off on some modern investment strategies—the same strategies Ben had used to build his own financial portfolio—then they'd have the capital to float their own loans. That was what Ben needed to move the company forward—capital to invest in newer technologies, to hire new workers, to build the company. Ben had a good head for numbers, and he had the well-balanced portfolio to prove it. He'd made millions by being careful.

Not that any of that mattered to his father.

Unfortunately, Dad would have none of it. Financial instruments weren't things Dad could touch. They were not to be trusted. Ben understood those financial instruments. Therefore, Ben was not to be trusted.

Still, it was part of the ritual to try. "Dad, we need to invest some of the—"

"Damn it, Ben, you still think I'm going to let a bunch of corrupt bankers take my money on a rigged crapshoot?" He slammed his fist into the desk, sending papers flying in all directions. "Hell, no. That's no respectable way to run a business. We do things the right way around here, or we don't do them at all, so stop asking me!"

"I know how to keep our money safe," Ben protested, trying to keep his tone professional. "Look at how well my investments have done. Bobby and Billy let me manage their investments, too—and we're all doing really well." Which was sort of an understatement—Ben knew not to get sucked into the next big thing, and he avoided the panic that had sunk the economy a few years back.

"We're in the black. The business is doing fine." Dad didn't so much say it as growl it. "We don't need any of that—" he waved his hands around "—money hocus pocus, or whatever you call it."

Ben refused to let his father's derogatory attitude get to him today. "It's called investing." He bit back the smart-ass "Everyone's doing it." Smart-ass never worked on Bruce Bolton. "The business is fine only because Billy, Bobby and I floated the company money to pay for this building."

"Your money? Ha! You wouldn't have any money if it weren't for your brothers. They do things. What do you do? Add, subtract. Mess around with numbers. I could get a fifth-grader to do your job. Your money..." Dad's voice trailed off in a chuckle. "My money is real. I can go to a bank and get cold, hard cash. Where is your money, huh? You can't even say it's on paper—it's all zeros and ones floating out *there*." He waved his had toward his computer.

Ben sat there, his face burning. He was so tired of this fight. No matter what he did—including paying for this fancy building—he couldn't get the old man to look at him with the same respect he gave Ben's brothers. "Look, if we at least investigated the possibility of bringing on some investors, besides us three boys, then we'd be able to—"

"That's enough! This is my business, boy, a fact you don't seem to remember. I'm not gonna tell you again. I make the decisions around here." Dad eyed him. "And if you have too much trouble remembering that, well..."

The threat was implicit. If Ben didn't toe the family line, he'd be replaced by a fifth-grader. Except, of course, that Dad would immediately discover how wrong he was. The temptation to quit and let the old man flounder was strong. Today, it was stronger than most days.

However, the moment he considered such a move, he heard his mother's voice in his ear as she lay on her deathbed. "Keep the family together, Ben. You're the only one who can."

His mother's voice had been weak, but he'd still felt the steel behind the order. His mother had been the only one who could keep the four Bolton men from killing each other, and Ben had promised that he wouldn't let her down.

So this was him not letting Mom down.

"I know who's in charge around here," he grumbled to Dad. He'd keep the company in the black—barely, but still black—the hard way. It was the only way to keep the family together. It was the only way to honor his mother.

He went back to his office and closed the door, shutting out the shop noise. This was the one room in the building where it was quiet enough to think. Ben sat with his head in his hands, wondering how much longer he could keep the business afloat and the family in one piece. Every quarter it got that much harder.

Then the corner of the brochure for the Pine Ridge Charter School caught his eye, and Ben's thoughts turned from stemming the hopeless Bolton tide to one Josette White Plume.

In the four days since Josey White Plume had kissed him and then disappeared, he'd found himself staring at the brochure on more than one occasion. He'd even checked out the website. Josey's name had been listed, but it hadn't seemed right to email whiteplume@prcharterschool.net about no-strings-attached sex.

But if he had some tools to give her, well, that would be a different story. A perfectly aboveboard reason to make contact, to see if that heat was still there, if strings were still unattached. To see if she'd been level with him about coming for the music.

The problem with that plan was that Dad would never let the company donate tools. Hell, some of those machines down there were as old as Ben was.

Just when things didn't seem like they could get any bleaker, Ben's office door swung open.

"Ben! My man!" Bobby barged into Ben's office.

Startled, Ben took the brochure he'd been looking at and shoved it under some paper. Great. His younger brother was back. Ben wasn't sure if that was a bad thing or a really bad thing.

Bobby plopped down in the guest chair and loosened his tie. He was the only one who wore ties around here. Anything to be irritating. "How was my nine-thirty? I heard she was something *sweet.*"

Ben ignored him. Rex and Bobby were pretty friendly, so no doubt Bobby had heard about the kiss. The question was, would Bobby put the nine-thirty and the kiss together?

"The silent treatment, huh?" Bobby whistled in appreciation. "She must have been something. What did she want?"

Me, Ben thought. *She wanted me.* "Donations. And thanks a hell of a lot for dumping her on me. It was quarter-end, you know. I barely got the reports done in time."

Bobby had the nerve to *tsk* him, as if Ben were some old fuddy-duddy to be pitied. "Come to New York with me next time."

"What the hell for?"

"For starters, you need to get out more. When was the last time you got laid?"

The pounding between Ben's eyes took on a dedicated rhythm. "None of your damn business."

"Ouch—not even that groupie? Rex said she was a piece of work." Bobby chuckled and slapped his hand on the desk. "Hard up, my man. Hard up."

"Shove it and get out. Unlike some people, I have work to do."

"Ben, that hurts." Bobby made a sad face at him, somehow managing to look exactly like their mother when she was disappointed in him. "Come with me in a few weeks and I'll show you what I've been working on."

"We can't afford it." Whatever "it" was, Ben was not footing the bill this time. Despite his best attempts, Bobby had not managed to do lasting harm to the company. Not yet, anyway. Ben couldn't help but feel that the whole business was just one Bobby-based incident away from financial ruin, and it fell to Ben to contain the youngest Bolton.

"Boy, the camera is going to *love* you, big brother." Bobby held up his hands like he was framing Ben for a shot. "Brooding, handsome, rich—"

Camera? Hell. Ben picked up the most recent bank statement—the one with all the charges from swanky New York hotels and martini bars—and flung it at Bobby. "Not that rich, thanks to you."

"That's all going to change, I swear. This deal—"

"No. No more deals."

"Yes." Bobby shot back at lightning speed. "I already talked to Dad about it."

The pain clobbered Ben in the forehead, the kind of instantaneous headache he imagined rhinoceroses got when they hit a brick wall going full tilt. Bobby's ultimate trump card—he'd already talked to Dad.

Ben felt like he was a kid again, back when he'd wanted to go to some science center on a family trip. Billy had been too old to care one way or another; Bobby had wanted to go to the zoo. Bobby had *always* wanted to go to the zoo, but Ben had wanted to see something besides pitiful animals.

He and Bobby had gotten into a big fight over it before Mom had broken them up. Ben had gotten a whipping while Mom had cuddled her "poor baby" and kissed the satisfying goose egg Ben had managed to get in on a parting shot. And after everyone had calmed down, Dad had glared at Ben and firmly announced that they were all going to the damn zoo.

Ben looked around his office. Was this any different from being a tiger on display, doomed to spend his life within these four walls, dying to get out and do something different?

Bobby was sitting there, grinning smugly at the victory. Ben should be used to this—losing the battle before he knew he was fighting one—but some things never seemed to change.

He looked down at his desk. The bottom half of the brochure was peeking up at him, with a map and directions to the school barely visible.

He made a snap decision. Bobby went to L.A.; Billy went on test drives. Ben wasn't going to spend the rest of his life staring at financial reports in this cage of an office.

It was high time Ben hit the road.

Josey surveyed the blanket of newspaper covering every possible flat surface in the multipurpose room. "Great job, girls." Twenty-seven faces beamed at her. "Now, who wants to stir the paint?"

"Me! Me! Me!" a chorus of little girls all shouted at once as they crowded around the cans.

Josey couldn't help but grin at them. The girls didn't care that the school wouldn't be done in time, or that she'd failed to get shop equipment. They didn't even care that the guy who'd promised her some band instruments had called this morning with some lame excuse about a "mix-up" in accounts payable, which meant her "free" trombones would now cost a cool thousand—unless she wanted to get together on, say, Saturday night and "talk" about her donation "needs" a little more. That kind of bait-and-switch wasn't uncommon, but it was as irritating as all get-out. Plus, she was still without instruments.

No, none of the kids—the girls clutching their cheap chip brushes, ready to paint, or the boys outside, hacking away at two-by-fours with half-rusted hand saws—cared about any of that. All they cared about was getting their very own school—and helping finish it.

Josey picked the two oldest girls, Livvy and Ally, to stir. As she crouched down to demonstrate how to pop off the lid, the hair on her arms stood up. Livvy made a noise that sounded like someone had poked her with something sharp. The rest of the room got very still, and the youngest, Kaylie, started to whimper. Josey looked up and saw everyone's eyes focused on someone behind her. She spun on her heels to see a tall white guy in black motorcycle clothes with dark hair and baby...blue...

Ben Bolton. Here. Now.

"I'll find you after the show."

He'd come for her.

Her mouth went dry as her eyes met his, which flashed with that dangerous desire again. Lord, he looked good. His cheeks were tinged red, his hair was mussed up and his eyes sparkled with mischief. And here she was, looking like she hadn't showered in two days. She'd fallen into bed after midnight and had been back out here at six this morning. Had she even brushed her teeth today?

"What are you doing here?" Her voice came out in a stutter. Excellent. She sounded as good as she looked. At least she managed to stand without landing on her butt.

One corner of his mouth moved in an upward motion. Was that a smile?

"I came looking for—" Kaylie squeaked and buried her face in Josey's overalls. Ben startled, as if he was realizing there were other people in the room for the first time. "The school," he corrected himself. "I came to look at the school."

In the awkward silence that followed, Josey found herself wishing that, for just once, she was ready when she saw this man. After the meeting at the bar, she wouldn't have thought she could be less prepared. Heck, she didn't even know what to say right now.

Ben looked around the room. The older girls were protectively standing in front of the younger ones; only the smallest ones were actually looking at him. "I'm sorry," Josey said, patting Kaylie's head. "They're not used to... outsiders." Which was the nicest way she could think of to say "white people."

Ben's cheeks got the tiniest bit redder. Oh. Blushing. Some of her panic melted into warmth. All kinds of hot.

"Hi, girls," he said with a cautious wave. At least he was trying not to be scary. She gave him a few extra bonus points for that. And the way his jacket fit his chest.

"Hey!" Suddenly, thunderous footsteps echoed down the hallway. "Who the hell are you?"

As if this situation could *get* any worse, Don Two Eagles burst into the room. Ben had the good sense to get the heck out of the way—without getting any closer to the kids.

"Hey, *wasicu,* what the hell do you think you're doing?"

That, in a nutshell, was why she should not even be *attracted* to Ben. God forbid, if she acted on that attraction, she'd run a real risk of having people like Don treating her just like this. A few of the braver girls giggled at the Lakota word for *white devil*—that, and Don's tendency to cuss no matter who was listening.

"Don," Josey said in her meanest polite voice, "this is Ben Bolton. He's here to take a tour of the school." She shot a glare at Ben for good measure. Although he didn't look the least bit concerned by this new development, he played along and nodded.

Don cranked his head to one side, cracking several joints at once. "Bolton? As in Bruce Bolton, the chopper guy?"

"That would be my father." Ben managed to sound cool, but he took a wary step back. A man like Ben Bolton wouldn't be afraid. He would, however, have a healthy respect for the situation. "You know him?"

Don cranked his head to the other side. More popping. "I broke my hand on his face back in '87." He unnecessarily cracked his knuckles, as if he wouldn't mind breaking his hand on another Bolton.

So that's why Don had argued so vehemently against her going to Crazy Horse Choppers in the first place. It was personal—going back twenty-five years.

"Sturgis? '87?" Ben didn't even look a little intimidated. In fact, the grin on his face said he was amused. "You're the one who broke his jaw? He was wired shut for a month after that. Most peaceful month of my life." Ben advanced on Don. Now it was the older man's turn to be confused. "Let me shake your hand, Mr...."

Don glared at Ben for a moment before he returned the grasp. "Don Two Eagles. I'm the shop teacher and coach." He looked at Josey as if to say, *what the heck?* All she could do was shrug. Now that she'd met the senior Bolton, she had to admit she was equally impressed that Don had knocked him down. Even if he had broken his hand doing it.

"A real pleasure." Ben seemed to mean it, too. He pumped Don's hand and gave him a hearty slap on the back. "Not too many men have put my old man down for the count." He chuckled, like this was some cosmic joke. "I'd steer clear of the shop if I were you, though."

"I ride Harleys," Don said, as if that would somehow make this whole interaction less weird.

Ben grinned, perfectly at ease. "Miss White Plume and I didn't get a chance to finish our conversation about donations for the school when we last met. I hope you don't mind me dropping by—I wanted to see the school for myself." He turned a huge, almost blinding smile to her. She barely recognized him.

It all sounded great—perfect even—but the buddy-buddy smile didn't match what his eyes were saying. His eyes were saying, I wanted to see *you*.

Her insides got a little melty.

"Yes—a tour." She forced herself to look away from Ben's contradictory face. "He wanted to be sure that we got what we actually needed."

Another lie—because she was pretty sure, from the way Ben looked at her, that what he needed was some wildly hot sex.

Don's wrinkled face was full of doubt. *"Wačhíŋmayaya hwo?"* Do you need me?

"Taŋyáŋ naúŋžiŋpe ló." No, we're okay. She felt bad about using Lakota in front of Ben—it was exceptionally rude—but the last thing she needed right now was Don to get his nose bent any further out of shape. Plus, the girls would be more comfortable with the stranger if Josey could keep things calm.

Don gave Ben the kind of look that made most white people pee their pants. *"Aawáŋič'iglaka yo."* Watch yourself.

Really? What was the point of threatening Ben if he was going to do it in Lakota?

Ben only notched an eyebrow, like he was thinking, *sure, you flattened my old man, but that was a long time ago*.

Josey cleared her throat loudly. "Thanks, Don, but we're okay," as if Don had offered to help. *Now get out,* she thought as she looked at him.

The big man gave Ben a departing glare before he left. Ben looked around and wiped imaginary sweat off his head—much to the amusement of the girls. Kaylie even managed a small giggle.

"So," he said, shining that hundred-watt smile on the room, "about that tour?"

"Yes. That tour." What she wouldn't give to have five minutes in the bathroom—alone—right now. Especially given the way that Ben was looking at her paint-stained overalls, her formerly white tank top and her frizzing braid. Heck, she'd settle for three minutes. "Well." She made a sweeping sort of gesture, barely clearing Kaylie's little head. "This is the multipurpose room."

God, those eyes—how could they be that blue?

"Multi?"

"Gym and cafeteria." She pointed to the tables at one side. An old elementary school was building a new cafeteria addition in Iowa and had been happy to let Josey haul the ancient fold-up tables and benches out free of charge.

"Music room," Livvy said in a whisper.

"Oh, yes. Thanks." Josey pointed to the one deer-hide drum in the corner. "And music room."

"What is that—a drum?"

Livvy sniffed in juvenile indignation. "A traditional drum," Josey explained, shooting him a warning look. She stepped into him, keeping her voice low. "Her father made it."

He nodded. "I've never seen one that, um, tall. Very impressive." Livvy rolled her eyes—but didn't cop any other attitude.

Josey fought the urge to stand there and gape at this man. He clearly had no idea what he was doing—but he was here anyway, trying to soothe a thirteen-year-old's ruffled feathers. He'd already talked Don back from the brink. He'd even convinced Jenny they were going to talk about the school in the middle of a crowded bar. Not to mention he'd survived the tornado that was his family. He was a peacemaker.

So why did he leave her so unsettled?

She watched as his unnaturally large smile faded, replaced with a look she recognized from their first meeting—

suspicious disbelief. "You have *one* drum for how many students?"

"Sixty-three." She couldn't help taking a deep breath. The smell of wind-whipped leather filled her nose, and she had the sudden urge to be out there on a bike with him, to feel the summer wind rippling through her hair. Not here on the rez, not at that war zone he called a shop. Someplace where she wouldn't have to worry about what anyone else thought of her—or Ben. "There's a problem with the instruments. Munzinga backed out of our deal."

A shadow fell over her face, and she found herself less than a foot from the all-businessman who'd flatly refused all of her offers. She didn't particularly care for the all-businessman. She kind of liked the drummer—not that she'd ever tell him that. He leaned over and whispered, "Munzinga? He's a jerk," in her ear.

So much for sweet nothings. Despite the insult, his breath touching her skin set off an unfortunate round of goose bumps—that she chose to ignore. "I figured that out yesterday, but thanks for the heads-up."

Thin lines appeared around his eyes, and his mouth did something that could be smiling—a real, honest thing. Whatever it was, the shadows eased back, and Ben went from hot to intensely handsome. His eyes moved over her face with exacting precision. "So, the multipurpose room."

"Just a second, and we'll go look at the shop." Josey left Livvy in charge of painting the walls and headed out into the hall. Ben followed—close, but not *too* close. Just within hand-holding range. Not that she would dare hold his hand within the same area code as Don.

The moment she opened the front door, the wind barreled across the hot grass, further demolishing her braid. "This way." She moved quickly through the grass before he could change his mind and bail on the tour.

The shop, if one could call it that, was a little ways off from the school. The bigger kids were sawing away at the two-by-fours while the smaller boys held the wood steady. Don saw them coming. Heck, everyone saw them coming—the whole lot of them froze.

"This is a concrete foundation." He seemed surprised about that.

"Classrooms have a higher priority than the shop."

"I guess." Josey pulled up short to look at him. Not what she'd expected to hear a valedictorian say. Ben shrugged, but they were within earshot of the still-motionless kids, so he didn't clarify.

Professional. Be professional. "Much like the cafeteria, this building will serve several purposes. In addition to housing the shop classes, we'll use it for storage and for the school vehicle."

"Why aren't they looking at me?" Crud. He'd noticed. "Do they have a problem with white people?"

How could she tell him that the only time most of these kids saw white people was when their parents were arrested for drug and alcohol violations? Or when social services came to take someone else away from the rez and the tribe—the only family most of these kids had? How could she possibly explain that some Lakota people refused to acknowledge white people at all—by not looking at them, they could pretend white people didn't exist?

How could she hope to explain that's why it was her job to be the face of the tribe to "outsiders"—because her grandfather had been an outsider himself? How some people still treated her and her mother like bastards at a family picnic? How some still whispered about her grandmother's "betrayal" of the Lakota Nation, all because she'd dared to fall in love with a white man? How it would never matter how much her grandfather had given to the tribe, because he would always be a white man from New York?

She couldn't. No one could ever understand how freaking hard it was to walk in both worlds—one where she was too Indian, the other where she was too white. She'd tried to explain it once—once, she'd been in love—and what had it gotten her? Nothing but heartbreak.

"No," she said, trying to keep herself together. "They're just not used to outsiders."

Ben regarded her with open curiosity, like he was trying his darnedest to make sense of this strange new world he'd casually wandered into. But she wasn't going to give him anything else.

He nodded. He was going to let it slide—this time. "Why are they using handsaws?"

Reality sucked. That's all there was to it, but that's not what she said. No, she was a professional, darn it. "I was attempting to negotiate for some power tools, but most shops operate on razor-thin margins and are unable to part with any equipment."

Ben's eyes narrowed as his nostrils flared. So maybe that wasn't the most professional thing she'd ever said. Too late. It was out there now, and there was no taking it back.

Josey gave Don the most meaningful look she had. The old coot seemed to get the message. He said something in Lakota under his breath, and everyone started moving again. They didn't look at Ben, but at least they weren't frozen in a workshop tableau.

"We should let them get back to work." She headed back to the building, but stopped short when she caught sight of the motorcycle. "Is that yours?"

"Built it myself," he said with obvious pride. "You like it?"

"It's beautiful." She'd looked at the Crazy Horse website,

seen all the wild bikes they'd be happy to build for a small fortune. But this bike was different. It had a vintage sensibility to it, with clean lines, a shiny gray body and normal-looking handlebars. Nothing like what was on his company's website, but very much Ben.

She looked from the motorcycle to the man. He was watching her. She cleared her throat. "Would you like to see a classroom?" Because they had only one that was done.

He fell into step with her. "What about you?"

She tensed. "What about me?"

"Do you have a problem with white people? With me?"

"With you being white? No."

He chuckled. "But you do have a problem with me."

Gosh, wouldn't it be nice if her mouth kept up with her brain? Yeah, she had a problem with him. More specifically, she had a problem with him just showing up when she least expected him. What next—he'd come to the house while she was in the shower?

She didn't want to admit that the white thing could be part of the problem. The way everyone—from Don on down—had reacted to Ben's mere existence made it perfectly clear that even entertaining the fantasy of another kiss would be fatal to her reputation within the tribe. She'd worked too hard to throw her place away on hot kisses.

She didn't meet his eyes. Instead, she cleared her throat and headed for Jenny's classroom. She was a professional, darn it. "This is our first- and second-grade room. Do you remember Jenny Wahwasuck? This is her classroom." She turned to look at Ben.

He was still standing in the doorway—filling it, really. He knocked on the drywall, flipped the overhead lights on and off, opened and shut the door.

She could just look at the man. He looked very much like he had when she'd first seen him—same belt, same boots, dark jeans, button-down shirt—but there was something different about him.

She couldn't put her finger on it until he turned those eyes to her. The danger—oh, he was still a dangerous man. But the only thing she was in danger of was losing her head.

He took a step into the room—just the one, but it sent ripples of energy around the small room. She realized that he'd shut the door. The sound of girls painting was a muffled waterfall of giggling in the background. "How many classrooms?" Another step. His jaw flexed, and she saw the cords in his neck tense.

Huh? What? Classrooms? "Um, four. Two grades in each."

"And when does it open?" He was only four steps away from her now—maybe three. He had long legs. Long, muscled legs.

"Twenty-three days." All she could do was watch him close the distance. All those muscles...

"Who's paying the teachers' salaries?"

The conversation was all business. The look in his eye was anything but. This couldn't be foreplay—could it?

"Mom and me—we manage the trust fund my grandfather left. We pay the salaries."

A confused look flashed across his face—not that it slowed him down any. "Kind of a funny feeling, isn't it?" He reached out and brushed a loose strand of hair off her forehead. "Having someone you're not sure you're ever going to see again show up in a place you didn't think anyone could find?" His fingertips didn't leave her face. They curved around her cheek and lifted her face toward his.

She swallowed. The intensity in his eyes was paralyzing her. "I can see how it would be unsettling."

"I told you I'd find you after the show." His breath danced

over her ear and took its time rolling down the back of her neck. Her skin broke out in goose bumps. "I looked for you."

She couldn't possibly let him kiss her, not in the first- and second-grade room. "Technically, this is still after the show. And I told you, I don't do one-night stands." She swallowed down her—what? Nerves? Desire? Both? "I don't screw guys I don't know."

"Hmm." His lips touched her cheek. The move was surprisingly gentle, even though his stubble pricked her face. "We could call this a third date. Does that count as knowing each other?"

Yes, her body screamed. The building heat between her legs was making her sweat, and her breasts ached for his touch. Oh, how she wanted to know him. Intimately.

But she couldn't. "No."

He didn't seem put off by that answer. If anything, he acted as if that was the one he wanted to hear. "How about a fourth date? No strings attached."

She could feel the deep bass of his voice reverberating all the way down to her core. He settled his other hand in the hollow of her back, just above her butt. She couldn't back away now if she wanted to. And she didn't want to.

This should be all kinds of wrong. The kiss at the bar had been wrong, too. But that was at a bar. She could claim that one hard lemonade had gone right to her head, or she'd been dazzled by the music. She hadn't been herself. Now? She had no weasel excuses to hide behind.

But she didn't care if it was wrong. He'd come for her. No one had ever sought her out before. No one had ever wanted her enough to risk a trip to the rez. To risk anything for her. Matt certainly hadn't risked anything for her.

His mouth took possession of hers—not a kiss, oh, no, nothing that simple. One moment she was struggling with what to say, and the next, he was consuming her. Her body responded, pulling him down into her. Even better, she thought as his tongue swept into her mouth. His hand somehow worked its way under her overalls and found bare skin. His fingers inched up, slipping beneath the band of her bra. His other hand did the same, except it went down, finding the breath of space between her panties and her bottom. And just like that, she was naked—while clothed—in his arms. In broad daylight. In the middle of a school.

Her knees fluttered—everything fluttered. Especially that hot spot between her legs. He could tell, too. His lips curved into a smile against hers while he hummed a satisfied sigh. She could feel the drumbeat of his heart against her chest, going faster and faster as the kiss deepened. Somehow, that sensation made her even weaker. He held her up, cupping her bottom, which made things better and worse at the same time.

God, if he touched her in just the right spot...

"Josey? Where are you, sweetie?"

There's nothing like the sound of a mother's voice to take the heated build of sexual tension and drive it into the dirt. Ben pulled away from her, taking up a safe spot across the room as Mom opened the door. "I've got lunch and— Oh!"

Just as he'd smiled in the face of a furious Don Two Eagles, Ben didn't even blink. He grabbed the grocery bag before it hit the floor. "Ma'am, let me help you with that."

Busted. Josey rubbed the back of her hand against her mouth, as if that would erase any sign of yet another stolen kiss. Good Lord, what was she doing? She couldn't even be sure if she'd brushed her teeth today.

Mom shot her a look of mild panic, which was enough to remind Josey what she needed to do. "Mom, this is Ben Bolton. He's the chief financial officer of Crazy Horse Choppers." Mom's eyes got even wider, as if to ask, *that* guy?

Josey nodded, yes—*that* guy. "Ben, this is my mother, San-dra White Plume."

"Ah—the principal? Nice to meet you." Still holding lunch, Ben managed a polite handshake. "Your daughter has been telling me about the good work you're doing here. I'm impressed at what you've accomplished."

Man, he was smooth.

Mom's panic turned to shock, but only for a second before she managed to pull it together. "Mr. Bolton, how wonder-ful of you to visit our school."

Josey took a slow, deep breath—in through the nose, out through the mouth. Mom's Lakota accent had dropped, and she spoke in her soft New York accent. She could just do that—turn off the Indian and turn on the New Yorker—like the flip of a switch. It always took Josey a little longer to switch gears.

"Sweetie?" Mom was looking at her. Josey realized she'd lost track of the conversation.

"Huh?"

"I said, I didn't want to *interrupt* your tour. Mr. Bolton, it is truly a pleasure to meet you."

"Ma'am, the feeling is mutual." Except he had that big, flashy smile on his face. He waited until Mom had reclaimed the bag of peanut butter sandwiches before he turned back to her. "But I do have to be going. Thank you for taking the time to meet with me today." And then he extended his hand for a nice, professional handshake.

Really? After he'd hunted her down—after he'd seen her at her grimiest—after *that kiss*—she was going to get a handshake?

Ben shook her mother's hand, too. Josey guessed he was thanking her, too, but her ears weren't working. Nothing was working.

Ben turned back to her. His eyes blazed at her. "Josey, I'll be in contact."

Her name. It was the first time he'd said it out loud.

The question was, what *kind* of contact?

Four

The clanking of the garage door sliding up snapped Ben back to awareness. He was at the shop? Funny. He didn't remember deciding to come back here. The last thing he remembered was...

Kissing Josey White Plume.

Damn. He'd kissed her. Again. This time had been different, though. He'd touched her. The heat of her bare skin still burned against his palms. Under his touch, her body had shaken with the kind of desire that couldn't be faked. The way she made him feel—it went way beyond not getting laid for a while. She drove him to distraction. If her mom hadn't barged in on them, there was no telling how far he would have taken her. How far she would have let him take her.

Not a mistake.

Was it?

"What are you doing here?" Ben's head shot up to find his older brother, Billy, standing in the middle of the shop, a muffler in his hand.

"I went for a ride today. She was pulling a little to the left." Ben rolled his bike into an open bay. "Been a while since I took her apart and put her back together."

So he hadn't consciously come back here. He normally changed the oil at his place. But getting his hands dirty and shooting the breeze with Billy was just what he needed to get that woman—that kiss—out of his system.

Billy shot Ben one of those looks and then smiled. It was probably a damn good thing the big man never shaved. No woman would ever look at Ben—or even Bobby-the-playboy—if Billy bothered to clean up. God only knew why he didn't. "Who is she?"

He ground his teeth. Was it that damn obvious? He stripped off his nylon jacket and dug out his coveralls. "No one. I just need to take better care of my bike."

Billy laughed at him. "Yeah. Right." But he had the decency not to press the issue. Instead, he turned back to the bike he was working on.

Zipping into his coveralls, Ben did a double take. The chassis of the machine Billy was working on was three-pronged. "I didn't think we made trikes."

Billy's normal glower settled back over his face. "We don't."

"So what are you doing?"

"*We* don't. *I'm* doing this on my own time." Before Ben could ask the most important question, Billy added, "And my own money, too. This has nothing to do with the company."

Ben didn't get anything else, and he didn't push. If he wasn't shouting at Dad, Billy rarely talked. Now that Ben thought about it, this was the longest yell-free conversation he'd had with his big brother in years.

Ben got to work. He'd built this bike with his own hands back in high school. He didn't care if the money was in wild choppers with crazy handlebars or Batman rip-offs with ultralow-profile tires. This bike was his and his alone. He knew exactly how fast it accelerated and decelerated, and exactly how fast he could bank a corner before he lost control. He had the scars to prove it.

He started with the oil while Billy worked in the next bay on his trike. "Who's the trike for?"

"What's her name?" Billy shot back a few minutes later.

"None of your damn business."

"Typical."

Ben ignored him as he took the carburetor apart. It was some time before he said, "What's that supposed to mean?"

Silence.

This was the difference between talking to Billy and talking to Bobby. Bobby slung words around like bullets and he had stocked up on ammo. So what if a few ricocheted away from him and he drew blood? So what if he never listened? Words were disposable. Meaningless.

Billy, on the other hand, hoarded words like they were gold coins. He could say three sentences in three hours and consider that a conversation. He thought about each and every thing he said, and he didn't say something he didn't mean.

True to form, it was another twenty minutes before Billy answered him. "The only time you come down out of your little cave up there and actually get your hands dirty, you've got woman problems."

Ben bristled. Maybe today, he liked Bobby better, because even though the little jerk said crap like this all the time, Ben knew he didn't mean it. "It's called an office. You have one, too. You should check it out sometime." Billy used his office for storage and sleeping. The shop was his office and everyone knew it. "You know you're behind schedule. Why the hell are you wasting time on that?"

Billy couldn't be goaded into a fight as easily as Bobby,

though. He merely snorted in amusement and kept working. Slow. Methodical.

"You remember Cal Horton?"

The silence had gone on so long that Ben had half forgotten Billy was still there. "Horton? The shop teacher in high school?"

"Yeah." Billy sighed as he wiped his hands on a rag. "He was like...the anti-Dad, remember?"

Ben nodded. Billy had lived in the shop class. If it hadn't been for shop, Ben didn't doubt that his brother wouldn't have graduated from high school. And Mr. Horton—Mr. Who, the kids had all called him behind his back—had been a scrawny guy with big ears, buck teeth and a voice that never shouted. Ben had taken shop for a while, but it was the one class in high school where he couldn't show up his big brother. After Billy, all the other teachers were thankful to have a Bolton who could be taught. But Ben always had gotten the feeling that Mr. Who would take Billy every day of the week.

"Anti-Dad. Very funny."

"I'm serious. He didn't make you earn his respect, you know? He gave it to you. To me, anyway."

The weight of thirty-two years' worth of effort to get Dad's honest respect suddenly crushed Ben's chest. "Yeah. I can see that."

"Cal helped me out a few times, when I got in real... trouble." Suddenly, Billy looked way more than serious. He looked positively moody.

Billy'd had no shortage of trouble back then. A smart remark about bail money and strippers danced around Ben's mouth, but a strange sort of sadness made Billy look young. Small, even—which was no mean feat. Let Bobby be the jerk in this family. Ben knew how to keep his mouth shut.

"Yeah?"

"Yeah."

Billy stood there for a moment. Ben was about to give him some space and get back to work on his bike when Billy unexpectedly went on. "After September 11th, he re-upped with the army, did three tours in Afghanistan before an IED got him a few years ago. He finally got clearance to ride again—but his wife doesn't want him on a chopper."

Hands down, this was the longest, heaviest conversation Ben could ever remember having with his brother. A lifetime of loyalty—what the hell kind of trouble had Billy gotten himself into back then?

Ben didn't even get his mouth open before Billy started talking again. "He expected better of me. Everyone else—even Dad—expected me to fail. But not Cal. He almost died for me, for my country. He never asked me for anything. The least I can do is build him a damn bike. On my own time. With my own money. And if you've got a problem with that—" His shoulders dropped and he swung his hands into loose fists.

"No, no problem." Ben threw up his hands in surrender. Only an idiot would push Billy.

"You don't look like an idiot to me." Josey's voice floated around his head as he and Billy went back to their respective bikes. Something else she had said popped into his head. *"People expect them to fail."*

One man had made the difference for Billy—a man who asked for nothing in return, but got unshakable loyalty anyway. Ben thought back to the little girls who'd been scared of him, the young boys who wouldn't look at him. Those kids—people expected them to fail. Was he one of those people?

Josey's face swam before his eyes. Not the polished businesswoman, not the hot chick at the bar, but her face today, with the big paint smear across her forehead and her hair crazy around her. He saw the warm, bright smile she had for those kids. She expected better of them.

She expected better of him.

Everyone expected so much from him—to keep Billy working, to keep Bobby in line. Dad expected him to fail, but also expected him to keep the company afloat. Not her. She didn't act like he had to have all the answers, like he was the one thing between her and complete, total failure. All she expected from him was to be something better. And all he'd done was kiss her.

He could do better. He could *be* better.

"Billy!" He had to shout over the air compressor.

"What?"

"You got any tools you don't use anymore?"

The dull pain in residence behind Josey's eyes picked up speed at an irregular clip. What a disastrous day. She could still hear Ben saying, "You have *one* drum for how many students?" Because one drum was all she was going to get.

At least she could take comfort in the fact that building the shop class from the ground up counted as real, live shop class. Maybe they'd postpone music class until after winter set in, when they couldn't do much on the shop anyway. Surely she'd be able to get some instruments in three months.

She could always try asking Ben—he was a musician, after all—but she'd already made up her mind about that. She didn't know what, if anything, was going on between her and Ben Bolton. She only knew that asking him for anything else would muddy the waters between pleasure and business.

Even if that meant no more kissing.

In this foul mood, Josey rounded the bend and slammed on the brakes. A massive, dual-wheel pickup truck—gray—with a custom trailer attached to it was parked next to the school. That wasn't the weird part. The weird part was that

the kids were swarming over both the truck and trailer, un-
loading box after box.

Josey did a quick mental check of her calendar. Nope—no
planned deliveries today. No more planned deliveries, period.
She didn't recognize the behemoth vehicle. What the heck?

Livvy came running the moment Josey opened her door.
"He came back!"

"He? He who?"

"That guy! He brought stuff!" With those helpful words,
Livvy turned around and took off for the truck. It was loaded
with boxes. Some were brand-new—circular saws, power
drills—and some were the kind of boxes a person scrounged
up for moving.

Shop tools? That guy? That was as much as Josey could
process before Ben Bolton himself strode back around the
building, talking to Don Two Eagles, of all people. Shock
stopped her short.

God, he looked good. Dark jeans that fit like he might as
well have been born in them, and a red chambray shirt—
cuffed to the elbows. He said something to Don, and the
older man nodded before barking out orders in Lakota. Don
was taking directions from Ben?

Power. Josey's blood began to pound. This was power so
real that she could smell it on the wind. Ben Bolton commanded absolute respect, and he got it—even from the likes
of Don.

And Ben had used his power to help her.

Livvy bounded up to him and pointed to Josey before
grabbing another box and taking off. His eyes met hers, and
he shot her a look that invited all sorts of contact. His long
legs cut through the grass as he headed her way.

Just once, I want to be ready for him.

That was all the thinking she could formulate before a
horn sounded behind her. She jumped and spun to see a van

pulling up behind her. The window rolled down and a guy who looked vaguely familiar leaned out. "Is this the school?"

"Yes?" It came out as a question, because, honestly, Josey wasn't sure of anything right now.

"Where do you want the instruments?"

"The what?"

"The instruments." A hand touched her in the small of the back, the fingers splaying out against the hem of her shirt before settling in. Speechless, she turned to see Ben standing next to her, a wicked grin on his face. He was touching her in full view of everyone. Including her mother. How could something that was so clearly a bad idea feel like it was the most natural thing in the world? "Stick, glad to see you didn't get lost."

"Says you," the man named Stick said with a raspy chuckle. "Where the hell am I?" His eyes turned back to Josey.

"Stick, this is Josey White Plume. Josey, this is Leonard 'Stick' Thompson, the guitarist in the band."

"Screw you." Stick flipped off Ben, but he was still smiling. "Call me Stick. Only my grandmother calls me the *L* name."

Josey tried to nod, but nothing seemed to be working. Not even her brain.

"What did you get?"

His hand still resting on her back, Ben leaned into the van. Josey had no choice but to lean with him. The whole thing was filled with black cases strapped down with bungee cords.

"Everything but a trombone, man. The only one he had was bent. Where do you want it?"

Ben had the freaking nerve to look down at her, as if she could put together more than two syllables in a sentence. All she could do was blink at him. His eyes flashed with something outrageously wicked. "Multipurpose room, right?"

"Uh-huh."

Ben's hand slid around to her side and he pulled her away from the van—and into his chest. "Just park by the steps in front and ask for Sandra. She'll get some kids to unload for you, okay?" Stick nodded and rolled toward the entrance to the school.

He was on a first-name basis with Mom?

Ben didn't let go of her. Instead, he leaned down to whisper, "I told you I'd be in contact." As his lips grazed her ear, her body shuddered with a rush of heat. Oh, that was contact, all right.

At least Josey had brushed her teeth today. And her hair was smooth and neat in a twist. She was wearing a business-appropriate dress with a jacket.

And all of her supply problems had been solved in the space of three minutes. By a man who made her all fluttery and melty at the same time.

However, she wasn't even sure she was breathing, she was so paralyzed with terror at this exceptionally public display of—well, maybe not affection, but familiarity.

No matter how good Ben's body felt against hers, this kind of touching was off-limits. Or it should be, anyway. What if people saw and, worse, what if they started making assumptions? What if this simple touch—okay, this *not*-so-simple touch—undid everything she'd worked so hard for?

Finally, her mouth opened. "Razor-thin? Margins?"

Lord.

Ben's chest—strong and hard against her back—shook for the briefest of moments. He was laughing at her. "Yeah, well, the business operates on razor-thin margins. My personal margins are not nearly as sharp—or as skinny."

His own money. He'd paid for all of this out of his own

pocket. Her mouth went dry. Of course she'd had a couple of people cut her a check before—usually out of a combination of pity and leave-me-alone contempt. This was different. She knew good and well that time was money to a man like Ben Bolton—and he'd spent both on her school. On her.

His hand left her waist and trailed across her back before finding her other hand. He stepped away. As if it were the most natural thing in the world, he laced his fingers with hers. "Come. See."

Beaming from ear to ear, Mom had kids emptying the van like it was a bucket brigade and the school was on fire. Clarinets, trumpets, amps, guitars, a complete drum kit—one piece at a time, a music teacher's dream come true—made its way into the school.

Ben let go of her hand mere seconds before Mom saw them and hurried over. "Isn't it wonderful, sweetie? Mr. Bolton—"

"Sandra, I told you to call me Ben."

The two of them grinned like they were on a second date, and Josey decided that she'd entered an alternate universe. There was just no other rational explanation for her mother to be smiling warmly at a white man, or Don to be following the same white man's directions, or a hard-rock guitarist to be handing out drumsticks like it was Halloween, for God's sake. None.

"Of course. *Ben* is just an answer to our prayers." Her mom turned shining eyes to him. "We cannot thank you enough for this."

"Sandra?" Stick called to her from the front steps of the school, and Mom excused herself. What next? Hell's Angels would swoop out of nowhere and finish the shop this afternoon, like an Amish motorcycle gang at a barn raising?

She grabbed him by the arm and hauled him out of earshot of the buzzing school. "What—?" At least that was a word, right? She cleared her throat and tried again. "What did you do?"

The corner of his mouth hitched up. The real smile. Boy, she was in serious trouble—but then, she already knew that.

"It turns out that Munzinga would rather not lose a valued customer such as myself, and he would prefer that word not get around that he's ripping off children. And he'd really prefer to keep all his teeth, so in order to make amends, he *volunteered* to provide a range of instruments for half off."

Ben had threatened Munzinga on her behalf? And then paid for the difference?

"Now," Ben went on, as if this were just another day on the rez instead of Christmas four months early, "some of those tools are secondhand from my brother Billy, but they're still all good. Billy sees the words *new* and *improved* and he thinks he's died and gone to heaven. The rest is small stuff—"

"Small?" A trailer full was *small?*

Something about his eyes changed, and he leaned down until he was less than a foot from her face, like he was daring her to interrupt him again. "Yes. Small. Things like band saws and planers take a little more work, and Don agreed that the shop building needs to be finished before those get delivered."

"Don agreed? With you?"

Just once, she wanted to be ready for this man, but nothing in her lifetime had prepared her for Ben Bolton on a mission.

Ben couldn't remember having more fun. Josey had no idea how delicious she looked right now. Her eyes were wild with shock, the breeze had tugged a few strands of that reddish hair loose and her mouth hung open. The only thing that kept him from closing those pretty lips himself was the audience of about fifty people—including relatives—all watching the two of them out of the corners of their eyes.

Hey, at least people were looking at him. More than five thousand dollars' worth of school supplies made a guy an instant insider.

He felt like laughing. For once, he didn't care about how much this cost. Anything was worth the look of stunned relief in her eyes—a burden lifted from her shoulders. The funny thing was, he felt lighter, like making things easier for her made it easier for him, too. Maybe part of that was the way distrust had changed to shock and then welcome the moment Don had realized Ben had come bearing gifts.

All he knew was that, right now, he wasn't the stick-in-the-mud trying to keep the wheels from falling off. All of a sudden, he was Santa Claus. It was an oddly satisfying feeling—something almost but not quite connected to the way his blood hammered into his groin when Josey looked at him with that mix of vulnerability and lust.

Like she was looking at him right now.

"Yes, with me." Maybe he'd kiss her anyway. No one would say anything. They wouldn't dare.

"I don't know how we can thank you." She swallowed, her eyes cutting down to his lips. "How I can thank you."

He could think of a couple of ideas—and that was just for starters. The stupid part of his brain tried to argue that he just needed a woman. That was all. But he was starting to think he didn't need just *any* woman. He was starting to think he needed *this* woman.

She looked up at him through those lashes again, her cheeks coloring a pretty rose. The sunlight caught the red in her hair, making her glow without a sequin in sight. He was pretty sure she'd glow anywhere.

Damn, he was screwed. He'd thought that move had been seductive in the dimly lit bar, but that was nothing compared to the impact of her beautiful light brown eyes in the full light of day. His body vibrated with the need to pull her into his arms, to feel her chest rise and fall against his—to know she only wanted to hear the band play.

"Let me take you to dinner—tonight."

Oh, yeah, he wanted her. But he wanted her to want him back. Just him. Not his money, not his band, not his financial skills and most certainly not his ability to keep the family together.

Her mouth parted, and she lifted her chin toward him. One kiss—what could it hurt? Idiot, he thought to himself as he moved closer. Like there was a shot in hell he could stop at just one.

"Benny!" The van honked behind him as Stick rolled up. "Setting a bad example again?"

The pretty went right out of Josey's blush as red embarrassment ran roughshod over her face. She took a step back. Ben glared at Stick. "Later? I'm going to grind you into dust, man."

Stick liked to laugh in the face of danger. Right now was a good example of that. "Whatever. Hey, I'm going to take off. We should hire those kids as roadies—they got the van unloaded in record time, man." He looked at Josey, unaware of how embarrassed she really was. A lifetime of bad bar behavior made him oblivious to the gentler ways of a woman. "Good kids. Maybe'll I'll come out some time and teach them some chords or something."

"That would be wonderful." She answered Stick, but she looked at Ben as she said it.

"Cool, cool. Hey, Benny—don't forget the gig tonight."

Damn. The gig. Now he looked like a total tool, inviting her to a dinner he couldn't make. She was thinking the same thing—he could see the disappointment of low expectations on her face.

To hell with this. He grabbed her by the arm and hauled her behind the relative safety of the van. "Come to the gig. It's at Fat Louie's."

Behind them, Stick wolf-whistled. Ben whipped his head up and glared at him. "Stick," he said in warning.

"Hey, man, um, look! Grass!" Stick turned his eyes to the front, although Ben could still hear him humming.

"Come tonight," he said again. Somehow, they were in the same position—her backed up against a wall, him pressing against her. God, the feel of her body against his... "I want to see you."

Again, she palmed his cheeks and pressed her forehead to his. "I can't," she whispered. Was he imagining things, or was her voice a little wobbly?

"Why not?"

"I have to go through all the things you brought—get them organized, cataloged, stored. I can't afford to let anything walk off. Not when you spent your own money... It'll take me a couple of days, at least."

Damn it all. He knew she was right, and part of him appreciated her treating his time and hard-earned money with respect. But that part was small and buried beneath a growing frustration. What did a man have to do to get a woman alone for more than two minutes? Or was this more her blowing him off now that she'd gotten what she wanted? He wanted to think she was different, but maybe he'd been wrong.

As if to highlight how uncomfortable his frustration was, she kissed him. A soft and gentle thing, her lips touching his—but it felt like so much more. Something inside him, something he couldn't pin down, shifted. It had nothing to do with the bottom line and everything to do with her.

"I wanted to make things easier for you," he said, his voice low and deep against her cheek.

Her chest hitched up, like she'd sucked in a bunch of air. "You did. You do. It's just…"

Yeah. Someone had to keep the wheels from falling off.

"Monday?" One of her hands had snaked around the back of his neck.

"Can't. Meetings scheduled with bankers all day. Same for Tuesday." Speaking of keeping the wheels from falling off… "Wednesday."

"That's the opening day of the powwow. The powwow!" Her body shot up against his, chasing most of the soft and gentle thoughts right out of his head. "You could come!"

No, really—what did a man have to do to get a woman *alone?* Because a powwow sure sounded a hell of a lot like more quality time with all of the people who were probably wondering where the two of them had run off to.

She must have sensed his hesitation, because she added, "There'll be drumming on the traditional drums, you know."

Well, hell. He had to admit he was curious about that big leather-and-wood thing in the multipurpose room, and it did seem to be the only way to see her outside of his office and her school. "Okay. I'll pick you up." So he didn't know where he was going. He wasn't about to let her drive him on something that was most definitely a date. "When and where?"

"Come to my apartment in the city. Here." She slipped free of his arms and dug around in her pockets until she came up with a piece of paper and a pen. "Can you be there by five?"

"One of the nice things about running my own company is I can be there whenever I'd like to," he said, more because it sounded good than because it was true. Some days, he felt like he was chained to the damn place.

A low whistle cut through the air. "Heads up, man—not that I'm looking or anything," Stick said with barely contained laughter.

Less than twenty seconds later, Sandra White Plume rounded the front of the van. Her gaze cut from him to Josey and back, but she just said, "Josey?"

"Hi, Mom." Man, that pretty blush was going to be the final nail in his coffin. But then, to his utter amazement, Josey went on, "So, as soon as I have that tax-deductible information for your records, I'll be in contact."

"Sounds great." Tax-deductible powwows?

"Mr. Bolton, we cannot thank you enough," Sandra began for the fourth time. "You must come to the tribal powwow this week—meet the people you're helping."

He looked at Josey, who was doing her level best not to laugh. How the heck had Sandra called that? "Sounds great. When does it start?"

"Wednesday." Sandra beamed at him. "I'm sure Josey can fill you in on all the details." She looked at Josey, and Ben almost heard her say, "If she hasn't already."

He wasn't fooling anyone.

Least of all Josey.

Five

The sound of the buzzer sent Josey jumping away from the mirror, her heart racing.

He was on time.

Even though she'd known the buzzer was going to ring, it had still startled the heck out of her. She shoved the clip into her hair and shut off the mindless TV she'd been trying to distract herself with. She tried not to run down the steps, but she was horrified to discover she was panting a little when she got to the bottom.

Cool, calm, collected, she thought as she took a deep breath and squared her shoulders. *It's only Ben—CFO, chief benefactor, rock star and all-around hot guy. No need to panic.*

Right.

She opened the door and about fell over her own feet. Ben had his back to her as he did something with his motorcycle. Why on God's green earth had she thought he'd be in the gray truck?

The door latched behind her, causing him to pivot. He was wearing his jacket and jeans again, but this time he had on sunglasses. Slowly, he took them off. A strange look crossed his face, and Josey briefly wondered if she had toilet paper stuck to the heel of her boots or not.

Then he closed the space between them in two long steps and kissed the hell out of her. In broad daylight. On the sidewalk.

Thinking stopped within moments as Ben traced her lips with his tongue. God, he tasted so good. As she met his mouth kiss for kiss, stroke for stroke, she couldn't even figure out what he tasted like—only that it was manly and good and *him*. The pressure of his hand in the small of her back seemed as natural as breathing, as did the feel of the muscles in his shoulders under her hands. Some parts of her got fluttery and some got melty, and the combination made her dizzy with desire.

When he pulled away, she wanted to cry. If something as small as a kiss could make her a kind of crazy that she couldn't ever remember being, what would sex with this man be like?

When she got her eyes open, his eyes—bluer today, but that had to be the late-afternoon sun—were staring at her, the corner of his mouth curled up. "Your mother isn't going to pop up out of nowhere, is she?"

"Your band isn't going to barge in?"

With a deep rumble, his chest moved against hers as a slow, easy grin spread across his face. Laughing. God help her. "I think that last time was a group effort." The grin faded as the look in his eyes intensified. "Just so you know, I'm going to kiss you again later."

She managed to swallow. Coming from him, it managed

to sound like both a threat and a promise. Mostly a promise. "I'm aware."

He gave her a quick kiss before he pulled her toward the motorcycle. He put the sunglasses back on, making it impossible to read him. "Good. You ever been on one of these before?"

"Nope."

Ben gave her a decidedly nonerotic once-over. "You'll be fine in those boots and jeans, but you should braid your hair."

So much for styling it. He leaned back against the bike and watched her as she plaited the braid, that strange look on his face. It felt like he was watching her undress. When she was finished, he hesitated and said, "I suppose we *have* to go to this thing, right?"

She wouldn't mind bailing. The whole concept of walking around a social event with him had her on edge. Would people think they were together? Would there be a scene? But she shoved those worries to the back of her mind as best she could. Mom had invited him; Josey was responsible for getting him there. That was that. "We should put in an appearance." That didn't seem to make him happy, so she added, "There'll be food."

"And drumming?"

"And drumming."

"Better be." For all the world, he sounded like a pouting child. She had to resist the urge to laugh at him. "But afterward, can we agree that there won't be any musicians or mothers around?"

Was being "with" him crossing a line—a line she couldn't uncross? Or would sex with Ben be something she could do—something she could *enjoy*—without losing all the ground she'd gained within the tribe?

She didn't know. But she wasn't turning back now.

* * *

"Of course," she said, her chin lifting up in what looked a hell of a lot like defiance. "After the powwow."

Damned powwow. "Good. Here. I brought you a helmet and a jacket. Even though it's hot, the wind can still get to you."

So Bobby's marketing decision to stock Crazy Horse Chopper jackets wasn't a total waste, and Ben appeared to have guessed right about the size. She zipped the snug leather over the tank top that had him wishing they could forget powwows ever existed. An appearance. Some food. Some drumming. That was it. Then, for the rest of the night, this woman was his and his alone.

He handed her the full-face helmet from a safe distance. It had taken every last ounce of willpower not to drag her up to her apartment and peel those tight jeans right off her. One more kiss—one more touch—would put him past all reason. Damn it, how was he supposed to drive anywhere with her sitting right behind him?

She took the heavy thing, the crease between her eyebrows getting deeper. "You don't need to worry. I rarely go more than ten miles over the speed limit, and I haven't had an accident in years."

"That's not exactly comforting." Her voice got muffled at the end by the shield on her helmet. She pulled it right back off, undid her braid and shook out all of that hair.

It was the most wonderful color of not-quite red, long and silky and begging to be touched. She looked a lot like the various people he'd met on his two trips to the rez, but her coloring was lighter. Not quite as light as her mother's—that woman was so fair as to be a strawberry blonde—but still exotic. Different. Special.

Not another woman like Josey White Plume on the planet.

She redid her hair, the braid starting lower against the

curve of the back of her neck. He stared at her with wide eyes as her fingers wove all that hair into a thick rope. She let the finished braid drape over her front, the tip swinging below the swell of her breast. This time, the helmet stayed on. Despite the leather and the helmet, she was still decidedly, unmistakably feminine.

Jesus. Would he make it to tonight?

Josey took a hesitant step toward the bike. The sooner they got this part over with, the sooner tonight could happen. "Just like riding a horse," he said as he snapped on his own helmet and motioned for her to get on behind him.

"Mmhmum hmmh mmumm."

Laughing, he turned around and lifted her visor. "What?"

"Not too fast," she said again, forcing a smile.

She was nervous. Was that because of the bike or because of him? "Not too fast. And you won't fall off if you hold on to me." Assuming, of course, that the weight of her body pressed against his didn't crash them both.

She bit her lip. "Okay." A woman shouldn't be as beautiful as she was. That was really all there was to it. "I'll, uh, point you where you need to go?"

He touched a gloved finger to her lips. "Anywhere you want to go, as long as I'm with you."

"Oh," she breathed, the pupils in her eyes widening considerably. "Okay."

They needed to get going. Kissing came after. Against his will, he flipped down her visor and fired up the engine.

As his machine rumbled to life, Josey threw her arms around his waist. Even though he'd known that was coming, his body stiffened at the sudden full-body contact. How long had it been since he'd had a woman on his bike? Since he'd made time to take a beautiful woman out for a ride on a sunny summer evening? Since he'd wanted to be with a woman bad enough that he'd suffer through meeting her family, much less a whole tribe of people?

Ben was in trouble, and he knew it. But as he accelerated toward the open road, with Josey clutching him to her chest and her helmeted chin resting on his shoulder, he couldn't figure out if it was good trouble or bad.

By the time they were on the highway, the sun setting over their shoulders, Josey had loosened up a little, which meant that she was only holding him tightly instead of crushing him. He'd take it, though. He made sure to stick near the speed limit.

A surprising thought hit him. He was having fun. Wind all around, his bike eating up the miles—sure, he loved all that stuff. But everything about it seemed better knowing that he was showing it to Josey for the first time.

Soon enough, she was pointing to an upcoming exit. Before long, they were on pea-gravel roads, and then onto things that were roads in name only. Just when he was sure they were lost in the middle of nowhere, the road opened up and ended around a huge site. Tents were pitched next to cars and lean-tos made of branches were next to horses. In the center was a wide circle ringed with lawn chairs and blankets. People were everywhere—kids running all over the place. Some people were in regular clothes, but some were wearing wild outfits, with feathers and colors sticking out in every direction.

He'd thought the school was a different world? This was a different galaxy.

Josey tapped his shoulder, pointing him toward a white van with the words *Pine Ridge School* painted on the side. Ben parked next to it.

He removed his helmet before he realized Josey was still holding on to him. After he pulled off his gloves, he ran his fingers over hers, prying them away from each other as gently as he could.

She let go and swung off the bike. Immediately, she stumbled backward. It was all Ben could do to grab her before she landed on her backside. "Whoa! You okay?"

Her head didn't so much nod yes or shake no as go in confused circles. Still holding her up, Ben got off the bike and then pulled her helmet off.

Her eyes were plate-wide. Then, to his great relief, her face cracked into a wide smile. "That," she said, her voice a little shaky, "was the scariest thing I've ever done!"

"Then you need to get out more."

Unexpectedly, she lurched up on her tiptoes and planted a kiss on him. He grabbed hold of her—to steady her, really—but she looped those arms around his neck and held fast.

God, what he wouldn't give to *not* be at a powwow.

As suddenly as the kiss had started, it ended. She jerked back, licking the lips he could still taste and wobbling for a short second before she landed firmly on her feet. Her cheeks burned bright red, and suddenly she couldn't meet his eyes. Hell, she couldn't meet anyone's eyes. Her boots had just gotten that interesting, apparently.

"Okay," she said, more to herself than to him.

"Okay," he agreed.

Wouldn't take much to be way more than just okay, but they were still in public, and she was clearly not comfortable with everyone around. He'd have to settle—for now.

Once he wasn't touching her, their surroundings registered. A deep, constant drumbeat filled the air around him, along with some singing that was closer to keening.

Off to one side, a group of guys were milling around, stuck between giving him the stink eye, ignoring him and staring at his bike. A motley crew of punks, some with Mohawks, some with long hair, all trying their damnedest to look intimidating.

They didn't look like the kind of kids who would hang around for formal introductions. So he cut to the chase. "You guys ride?"

The kids shifted, as if they were discussing whether or not to acknowledge him. This "outsider" thing was starting to really bug him. Finally, the tallest kid—one of the long-haired ones—broke rank. "We ride war ponies, *wasicu*."

Josey's shoulders dipped, like this pronouncement disappointed her, but Ben found the attitude to be amusing. Did this kid think he was intimidating? Please.

Ben made a mental note to ask Josey what *wasicu* was— he would guess "white guy," but he had a feeling there was another meaning to it. "Yeah? How do those handle on the highway?"

A chunkier guy with shorter hair cracked a grin and punched the leader in the shoulder. "Hey, the *wasicu* is funny! Where'd you get that thing?"

"I built it."

"No way!" The group began to edge toward him, although the leader was still scowling.

Questions began to come at Ben like arrows. "How'd you do that? How fast does it go? Do you get a lot of girls?"

At that last one, the rest of the group fell silent. Ben glanced at Josey, who was somewhere between mortified and amused. Ben chose his words carefully. "I built this when I was in high school. When most guys were trying to borrow their dad's car, I had my own bike. Because there's a lady present, I'll just say that Saturdays were the best day of the week." She shot him a look that said, *I bet,* as loud and clear as if she'd spoken it.

"Cool!" Even the leader was edging closer as the guys began to talk in a mix of English and Lakota. Ben didn't catch half of what they said, but he did hear someone say, "Like a two-wheeled war pony, Tige!"

"Josey," the chunky one said, "can we build one at school? Don would let us in shop, wouldn't he? Like a school project, right?"

Everyone turned to look at Josey. Her mouth opened and shut once, then twice as the color on her cheeks deepened.

"You've got to get the shop finished," Ben said for her. He crossed his arms and leveled his best glare at the kids. "If you can't build a building, you can't build a bike."

"Tige, Corey," Josey said over the resulting chatter, "don't you have to get your outfits on?"

The group of guys moved off, some still pointing to the bike. Not too bad, Ben thought. He still didn't know what *wasicu* was, but at least everyone could agree—a good bike made the world a better place. He turned to look at Josey, expecting to see the same sentiment on her face. Instead of appreciation, she had her hands on her hips and was giving him *the look*.

"What?"

"Saturdays are the best days, huh?"

"Were. Past tense." Her toe began to tap. She wasn't buying it. "Okay, so Saturdays are still the best days, but that's because of the band." She still didn't look mollified, so he added, "Recently, though, Wednesdays have begun to look up."

"You can be quite charming when you want to be, you know." He couldn't tell if she meant that as a compliment or not. Then her eyes cut to someone behind him.

He braced himself for another confrontation—who was going to call him *wasicu* now? But instead of a glowering Indian, a blondish boy who was maybe fourteen stood behind him in a full pout.

"Jared? What's up, buddy?" Josey's voice took on a soft, motherly tone as she stepped around Ben and went to the kid.

"They're calling me *it* again." The kid was way too old to sound like he was on the verge of crying, in Ben's opinion. "The girls won't even talk to me."

"Oh, sweetie." Josey put her arms around the kid's shoulders and gave him an awkward squeeze. "We discussed this. You can't let them get to you."

"What?" When Ben spoke, both the boy and Josey looked up at him like they'd forgotten he was there. "What's the problem?"

"Tige and his gang call me a half-breed," the boy said as he rubbed his nose on the back of his hand. "No one likes me."

"That's not true. Seth likes you."

"That's because he's your cousin. The girls all laugh at me."

Ben could not stand here and watch this kid cry. It wasn't dignified. Josey might be trying to help, but she was in serious danger of smothering the kid with pity. "Look, Jared, right? You're going about this all wrong."

The kid looked up midsniffle. "Huh?"

Ben grabbed him by the arm and pulled him away from Josey's misplaced sympathy. "You want girls to like you, right?"

The kid shot Josey a terrified look. "Yeah?"

"Then you've got to *be* someone they want."

"But I'm—"

"Doesn't matter what you are or aren't. Girls want what they can't have. You've got that wounded, sensitive thing down, but whining like a baby about how no one likes you? You're killing any mystery. You," he said, poking the kid in the chest, "don't go to them. You make them come to you. You don't give a damn if they want to be your friends or not."

"Language!" Josey scolded behind him.

Ben kept going. "You don't need anyone, okay? You're better than them, and you know it. Everything you say and do should convince people it's true. Look, I know what it's like when people expect you to be this or that and you're not any of those things." Boy, did he know. "But you can't let them define you. You have to define yourself. That's how it works."

The kid looked less terrified and more confused. "But won't that make girls like me less?"

Was it possible that Ben had been this clueless back when he was a squirt? Lord, he hoped not. "Once girls think you don't want them, they'll be curious—why don't you want them? What's your secret? If you're doing it right, they'll get it into their girl brains that you should share your secret with them, because only they can take away your pain. Girls like a challenge."

For a second, the kid brightened up, but then his face fell again. "But I'm—"

"No buts. And you're what, fourteen?"

"Fifteen," the kid said with a flash of anger.

"Hey—that was good. Keep that anger. Drives girls wild. And what about that— Who was it, Josey? The one who's father made the drum?"

"Livvy?" The look on her face was one of pure horror.

Ben ignored the horror. He was actually having a little fun. "Yeah. She was cute. What's wrong with her?"

The boy rolled his eyes—something he'd clearly practiced. "She's, like, eleven, mister."

"Listen, *kid,*" Ben said, trying not to smile. "Give her a few years. Some girls are worth the wait. Until then, watch some James Dean movies and practice being the lone wolf, okay? Pick a few fights, take up a dangerous hobby, stop doing *that* to your hair," he said, waving to all that styling gel, "and for God's sake, stop sniveling. Chicks don't dig wimps. They dig bad boys."

The kid had definitely stopped sniveling. "You really think it will work?"

"I don't think. I know. When you know who you are, everyone else will want to know, too. And when you're sixteen, maybe we'll get you on a bike, okay?"

"Really?" The kid flipped his hair out of his eyes, puffed out his chest and adopted what was probably supposed to be a look of disdain. "How's this?"

"Good start. Keep trying."

"I'm going to go tell Seth! Thanks, mister!" He took off like a shot.

Ben watched him go. "Kids," he said to himself.

"Men," Josey countered. She wasn't smiling. "Pick a few fights? Take up a dangerous hobby? Really? He's just a boy."

She could try to be mad at him, but he wasn't buying it. "A boy who needs to figure out how to be a man. So he gets a few black eyes—it'll be good for him. You can't coddle boys. The sooner he learns to fight for what he wants, the better off he'll be."

Josey stared at him. He had no idea what she was thinking—he was a jerk? He'd permanently damaged that kid? "Besides," he added, "I thought you liked the ride."

Finally, her face relaxed into a rueful smile. "I'd argue with you if you weren't so right. Come on."

He walked next to her as she threaded her way through the crowd. It wasn't that difficult—people got out of the way with feet to spare on either side. He looked around. Not too many "outsiders" were around. He picked out Josey's mom at a hundred paces. As they closed the distance, he noticed that people were quick to smile and exchange a few words with the older woman, but no one stayed long—and no one was sitting near her. It was almost as if she had a demarcated line around her that no one dared to cross.

Again, he wanted to ask what the deal with that kid had been, but he picked up the scent of fried bread and beans and meat—venison, he'd guess—about the same time the drummers kicked the beat up a notch or two.

By the time they reached Sandra White Plume's blanket, a hush had fallen over the crowd. "You're late," the older woman whispered.

"Got sidetracked with Tige and Jared."

Sandra looked mortified. "They weren't fighting, were they?"

"No." Josey shot him a look that might be admiration, but it was gone before he could tell for sure. "Ben talked to them."

Sandra looked like she might kiss him. "Mr. Bolton, you're becoming quite the savior to our little school." Luckily, instead of a smooch, she handed him something that looked a little like a soft taco.

"Fry bread taco," Josey said, getting one for herself. "I'll take you over to the drums after the opening dance, okay?"

He could only nod, because he was already halfway through the fry bread taco. Salty and spicy and greasy— this wasn't health food by any long shot, but it was a whole bunch of good. *Taco* was a lousy name for this, because he'd never had a taco anywhere near this good.

Josey was chowing down on hers, too. For some reason, that made him smile. He didn't like women who picked and poked at dead lettuce before taking "a bite" of his dessert because they weren't going to "eat a whole one" themselves. He liked a woman who wasn't afraid of food.

The drumming intensified, and some dancers began to make their way into the ring. "Grass dancers—they flatten the grass for everyone else," Josey said, hiding her full mouth behind her hand.

Ben nodded as he chewed. Sure, the outfits were crazy—feathers everywhere, ribbons and more mirrors than he would have guessed—but the rhythm was tight and the men in the ring were keeping the beat with their feet on the ground.

As the song went on, the moves the dancers made got more frenzied. They swung wider, jumped higher and landed harder. It should have looked like a mosh pit with better accessories, but Ben found it almost beautiful. He ate a second fry bread taco and bobbed his head in time with the music.

Suddenly, the beat paused—and the dancers stopped, too, crouching down in low positions that made it look like they were stalking something. Then it kicked back up. Josey leaned against his shoulder and whispered in his ear. "It's a competition. Better score for stopping with the music."

For a second, he forgot about the dancers, the drummers and the tacos. All he could think about was the feeling of her weight leaning against his, of her warmth touching the side of his face. He turned to look at her, and their eyes met. Heat flashed through his groin as she blushed and looked at him through her lashes.

Yeah, he was having a decent time. Fun, even.

But he couldn't wait to get her alone.

Six

Don was drumming, so Josey felt okay leaving Ben in the drum circle for a few minutes. He seemed comfortable—sitting on his heels, rocking in time to the beat, a boyish grin on his face. He was too good-looking to pull off cute, but right then, he came darned close.

She hurried back to Mom's blanket. "Remember, I'm not coming out tomorrow. I've got that meeting at ten at the University of South Dakota about certification." Which was true. But Josey felt the need to have an iron-clad reason she wouldn't be out on the rez at the break of dawn that had nothing to do with waking up in Ben Bolton's bed.

Don't get ahead of yourself, she thought as Mom's eyebrows notched up with uncontained suspicion. She didn't know for certain that she'd be waking up with him.

"That's fine, dear." Mom looked back across the circle and past the fancy dancers to where Ben was now handling a drumstick alongside Don. "He seems like a good man."

Josey relaxed a bit. They'd let Ben sit at the circle; Mom gave all indications that she approved of him. Heck, he'd won over some of the toughest kids on the rez. Maybe she'd been wrong to think that Ben would be excluded—and, by extension, that she would be, too. "I think he is."

For a hard-rocking, bike-building tough guy who cursed like a sailor, he seemed to have a fundamental core of decency.

She gave her mom a peck on the cheek. "See you in a few days."

Mom caught her in a quick hug. "Have fun, and be careful."

That was a perfectly normal Mom thing to say, but it hit Josey a little differently, as if Mom was giving tacit approval to the wanton carnality that Josey hoped was coming. Again, Josey wondered if that was because Mom liked the man, or because he had so easily stepped into the role of savior for their little school.

Not that it mattered. She would like to have some good, old-fashioned, man-on-woman fun. And she'd rehearsed her must-use-condoms conversation in her head. She could sleep with him without it getting too serious. She was good to go.

Ben was watching her as she made her way back to the drum. She could feel the energy sparking off him as he held her gaze literally without missing a beat. He didn't belong here—this wasn't a show powwow for the tourists, but a real one for the tribe—but between Tige, Jared, Mom and now the drum circle, he seemed to fit in just fine.

A lifetime—two lifetimes, if she counted Mom—of struggling to be accepted by her own people, and they were already welcoming him with open arms. Mom loved him, but Josey found herself wondering how Dad would have felt about this outsider.

The strangeness of the whole situation caused her step to

falter. Was it just because of the money Ben had been throwing around? Grandpa had money, too—but when his back was turned, everyone talked about the wannabe *wasicu*. Was it the way Ben commanded respect? Maybe it was like he'd told Jared. *You don't go to them. They come to you.*

Maybe she had it wrong. Maybe this was exactly like it had been for Grandpa. Maybe once they left, everyone would sit and gossip about how Josey White Plume was so white she couldn't get a decent Lakota guy and had to take up with a *wasicu*. True, he was a *wasicu* with money—but had he earned their respect or bought it? What would happen when the money, the things, stopped rolling in? Would Ben—would *she*—be less welcome?

She turned a slow circle. No one met her gaze. The throbbing in her head did not keep tempo with the drumming. She'd worked for so long to earn her place at this circle—would she really throw all that away for a white man? Even if that man was Ben Bolton?

What was she doing here?

Ben hit a downbeat before backing out of the circle, Don seamlessly taking up his stick. Everyone nodded to everyone else. No hint of malice, no kissing up. It looked so normal.

Ben walked toward where she'd stopped, his eyes focused on her. He didn't care about what everyone would or would not be saying after they left. She could tell by the way he moved, a coiled confidence underneath his easy gait.

When he got close to her—not quite touching, but close enough—he said, "A little dancing, some food, a little drumming. I think I've seen the powwow."

"We should go." Go home—with him. *Sleep* with him. Was this what she wanted? Was this what she should do? Would those two things ever be the same thing?

She needed to get away from the confusion that was threatening to swamp her.

Ben looked her in the eyes, his concern obvious. No, she didn't want to see anything that even hinted at pity, so she turned and walked back to where the bike was. Thankfully, no one was around, although there were enough footprints in the dust to let them know that plenty of people had been snooping.

"Where to?" Ben said.

Most men wouldn't have asked. Most men would have just headed for the nearest bed and taken what she'd more or less promised. If Josey had learned anything, though, it was that Ben wasn't most men.

She needed to get her head back on straight, and there was only one place in the world where she could do that. "There's someplace I've got to show you first."

Yeah, the powwow hadn't been nearly as miserable as it could have been. Don had even let him get in a few licks on the biggest drum he'd ever seen. The dancers had been cool. The tacos were awesome.

Something about Josey had changed, though. By the time he'd gotten back to her, she'd seemed further away from him. He wanted to take her home—but he wanted her to *want* to go. So when she said she needed to show him something, he went along for the ride.

They left the powwow far behind, but instead of heading back toward civilization, they went deeper into the middle of nowhere. After twenty minutes, he was navigating something that was little more than a deer path in the grass.

It had been a long time since he'd taken his bike this far off road, but thanks to the dual-sport tires, the terrain wasn't a problem. They were coasting around the bottom of a long line of hills. To his left was a sea of brown grass. To his right was a stand of pines that rose a good ways over their heads and seemed to go on forever.

He'd lived his whole life in South Dakota—except for college in California—and he'd never seen this side to the state. The contrast was stark, but that only made it more postcard-pretty.

Josey tapped him on the shoulder and pointed to a draw up ahead. He rolled to a stop.

"Where are we?"

"Nowhere" was all she said as she shed the jacket and helmet. Her voice was quiet. Hollow, even. Like she was seeing a ghost. Before he could respond, she'd climbed the draw and disappeared behind the trees.

"Josey?" he called out as he made his way through the forest. The pine-fresh smell was a thousand times stronger than that stuff Cass used to clean the office. The place was a sort of noisy quiet—birds chirping, wind rustling—but the overall effect was one of silence. No manmade noises, he realized. At least, none now that he'd turned the bike off. He pressed on, trying to catch a glimpse of her. Where was that woman?

The trees opened up, and Ben found himself on top of a bluff that overlooked a river and a wide, deep valley.

Josey was sitting on a huge boulder, her arms curled around her knees—something that was sensuous and natural while also innocent and sweet, even. Clearly, she'd sat like this before. *She belongs here,* Ben thought. No business suits, no schools.

"Josey?"

She didn't move, and Ben didn't feel quite right about interrupting the moment. Instead, he focused on where he thought she was looking. In front of him was a view bordering on spectacular—miles and miles of nothing but Great Plains. Part of him would have been happy to just sit here with her and watch the world spin. The other part wanted to know what the hell was going on.

"This was my grandmother's place," she began with no other warning. "They lived in New York during the school year, but they came back to the rez for Christmas and the summer. She would come here first so she could get right with the spirits."

What was he supposed to say to a statement like that? He decided the best course was to say nothing. The wheels in his mind were spinning fast, though. New York—*that's* what Sandra's accent was. Josey's wasn't as strong, but if he remembered right, she'd said her MBA was from Columbia. He'd just assumed she'd grown up here on the rez. And was this the same grandfather who had left her in charge of a trust fund?

"I remember she'd swoop me up on a horse, and we'd go flying over the grass." Josey's voice was far away. Either that, or the ghosts were really, really close—because Ben got the distinct feeling that spirits were hanging around. "That's what it felt like, anyway. *Flying*. She'd hold me up on the rock and say, 'Never forget who you really are, Josey-girl.'" Josey gave Ben one of those vulnerable smiles. "She called me that. Josey-girl."

"She loved you." Man, he hoped that was an appropriate thing to say. Talking was not something that usually happened in great quantities on his dates. Maybe that was why he hadn't been on one in a while.

"She did." Josey uncurled and stood on the rock. Ben couldn't help but watch as she stretched out, her lithe form close enough to touch and yet still so damn far away. "Grandma, she walked in both worlds and loved them both."

What did that mean, walked in both worlds? Was that code or something? Before Ben could ask, Josey turned to him, her eyes a little brighter at the memory. "She took me to the Met my first time, and the Statue of Liberty, before she got sick. I have a picture...." She trailed off again, and turned her eyes back to the vista in front of them. He saw her swallow. A minute passed before she said, "Mom couldn't do it. She never belonged to that world. She tried once, but she doesn't talk about it. So she married a Lakota warrior and came back to the rez. Permanently."

Ben was pretty sure he'd remember meeting a Lakota warrior. He pictured someone a lot like Don, but with more feathers. "What happened to him?"

"He died. A long time ago." Her voice was flat. She didn't elaborate.

"Yeah. My mom…" Even though it had been a long time—sixteen years—it still hurt. Time had taken the sharp edge off the loss, but dull pain was still pain.

"Yeah." Josey took a deep breath and stretched out her arms, like she wanted to hug the wind or something. Maybe the wind was looking for a hug, because it picked up the pace and started to blow with meaning. "I try. I really do. When I'm out there, I smile and nod and ignore the people who laugh because my last name means I'm not white enough. And then I come home, and I smile and nod and ignore the people who laugh because my hair, my mom's hair, means we're not Indian enough."

People laughed at her? A surprising anger hit him in the gut. Who cared what her last name was, or what color her hair was? Who cared if her granny liked New York or her father was a warrior? He didn't. What he cared about was protecting the woman standing before him from the small-minded people of the world. She was too sweet, too gentle, too damn *good* for people to laugh at her.

He was about to say as much when she turned to him, her eyes wide open and knowing. "I still come here when I need to remember who I am."

"Who are you, really?"

"You know what? No one ever asks me that." She stepped down off the rock and stood on the edge of the bluff.

"I'm asking."

A breeze came up the side, doing sexy things with her hair. He couldn't help it. He took a step toward her.

She shot him a mysterious smile over her shoulder. Whatever distance she'd put between them seemed to blow away with that breeze. "Maybe that's why I like you."

His blood began to hammer in his veins. Maybe he understood what she was saying about walking in two worlds and remembering who she was—maybe he didn't. He could understand never being what people wanted him to be, because he was never going to be Billy and he was never going to be Bobby and no matter how many gigs he played or how well he managed the money, he was never, ever going to be someone his father could be proud of. He would never be the son his father wanted.

What he knew for sure was that this place was special to her, and she'd brought him here. Because he was special to her.

When he slipped his arms around her waist, she leaned back into him without hesitation and laced her fingers with his, just under the swell of her breasts. His chest rose and fell against her back and he rested his chin on her head.

In that moment, Ben felt the way he'd felt in the bar, only in reverse. The solitary quiet he usually felt was less solitary, replaced instead with a gentle calm. He understood how alone Josey felt surrounded by her tribe, how hard it was to try and try and try and never be enough, how tired she was of doing it by herself. He understood it all and was happy to take some of the burden off her shoulders.

"Maybe that's why I like you, too." He whispered the words in her ear, but they seemed to echo over the bluff and into the grassland below.

She took a deep breath, her chest expanding against his arms. Together, they took a small step away from the edge. He couldn't help it if his arms tightened around her, if his hands splayed out so he could feel more of her. He couldn't help it if the way her hips moved against him made him think thoughts that had nothing to do with the sacredness of this place. He couldn't help wanting her.

"Do you like me?" She pivoted in his arms and, palming his face, looked him in the eye. "Do you?"

What kind of question was that? He'd suffered baptism by fire in meeting her mother and her tribe—on multiple occasions—and she had to ask if he liked her? Women, he thought to himself as he let his lips do the answering for him.

He took his time tasting her. No mothers, no bandmates—nothing but the breeze was around to watch her run her fingers through his hair, or to see him pull her shirt out of the back of her jeans so that he could get his hands on her bare flesh. She responded by shimmying those hips against his.

He could do sex in the wide-open spaces. Hell, given the way she was sucking on his lip, he was pretty sure he could do sex anywhere. Certain parts of his anatomy jumped to agree. Anywhere, as long as it was with her.

He had her top half off when she pushed him away. "We should go."

"Where?"

She closed her eyes and licked those lips. "Your place," she said as she grabbed the edge of her shirt and pulled it back down. "Take me to your place."

Seven

The motorcycle seemed to go faster and faster, until the world around her was nothing but a blur. They couldn't be on the highway anymore. They had to be flying, faster and lower than she'd ever flown before. For a lost second, she felt like the little girl she'd once been, flying on the back of a horse headed to the place where she could be herself.

Except she wasn't, not anymore. Now, she was a grown woman going home with a grown man. That's what she wanted right now. To hell with what anyone else thought. She may not have the best idea of who she really was, but Ben was the only man to ever ask—and that's who she wanted to be with.

She clung to Ben, every part of her front touching every part of his back. The motorcycle hummed between her legs, making it hard to breathe. *Faster,* she thought. *Go faster.*

Finally, the blur became streaked with light. Josey took that to mean they were near the city, but she couldn't make out anything else.

She clung to Ben, trusting that he knew how to ride this machine. This whole thing was perfectly safe. There was absolutely no reason to be panicked about any of this. Least of all the fact that Ben was driving like a bat out of hell so he could take her to bed.

Despite the body-tingling vibrations shaking her to her core, she could feel his heart hammering away underneath his jacket. Yes, she was a little nervous about this. It had been far too long since her last lover. But the feel of her arms around his broad chest and the way his last kiss still burned on her lips was enough to push her past her worries.

To be wanted was a satisfaction in and of itself. Ben wanted her so bad that the world was a blur. He couldn't wait, and truthfully, neither could she.

The world stopped spinning as he slowed down and made a series of turns. Soon she could even make out her surroundings—large warehouses in an industrial neighborhood. Ben brought the bike to a fast idle when he pulled up alongside a nondescript building. He punched a button, and a steel door rumbled up. He walked the bike inside and pushed two more buttons. The steel door slid down, and moments later the whole floor was lifting them up.

"Where are we?" she asked, finally venturing to unlock her arms from around his waist now that the bike was no longer hurtling in a horizontal direction—although she found the vertical a little disconcerting. Who had an elevator big enough for a motorcycle in their house?

"My place," he said, unstrapping his helmet. He put the kickstand down and waited, but Josey wasn't sure she trusted her legs right now. After a second, he slid off without knocking into her. He took her helmet off for her. "Also known as the former headquarters of Crazy Horse Choppers."

He lived in the old factory? Visions of a place that looked exactly like that stainless-steel office—only with a bed in

it—flashed before her eyes. Was there anything even re-
motely sensual about stainless steel?

The freight elevator—for that's what it was—lumbered
upward. They passed the second floor. A heavy bass beat cut
through the gauzy red fabric that covered the elevator shaft.

Ben caught her confusion. "I rent the second floor to a
couple of artists. They clean my place twice a month, and
I let them pay me in paintings when they can't make rent."

"Really?" He was an art patron? Maybe that wasn't so far
off from savior of the school. "Who else is here?"

He stepped closer to her and unzipped her jacket, the
edges of his fingers grazing the inner curves of her breasts.
Vibrations—different from the mechanical rumbling that
had burned between her legs—caused her upper body to
tremble. The corners of Ben's mouth curved up. He'd noticed. "The first floor is the band's—storage, practice. Been
thinking about building a recording studio in there…Billy
uses the third and fourth floors to store all his old bikes. And
I live on the top floor."

Two entire floors of emptiness separated him from the
rest of the world. And now that her jacket was unzipped,
she was just that much closer to naked. In a freight elevator.

He leaned in, one hand on the seat in front of her, the
other behind her bottom. He wasn't touching her, but only
by millimeters. Otherwise, he had her most intimate areas
surrounded. The tip of his nose brushed against her forehead,
then down to her ear. "Did you like the ride?"

"Seemed fast." Like speed-of-sound, life-flash-before-
your-eyes fast.

His lips caressed her neck. "I can do slow, if that's what
you want." He shifted, and he went from not touching her
to touching her—a small difference, but one that sent shock
waves through her center. One of his fingers was between
her and the leather seat. She gasped when he moved again—

the smallest movement possible, but one that hit that secret spot in just the right way. "Very slow," he murmured, his lips tracing the curve of her jawline.

A bed? Who needed a bed? Josey pushed his jacket aside and dug her fingers into the swath of muscles he called shoulders. Ben exhaled extra hard against her skin and rolled his hand so that he was cupping her. Tightly.

Her body bore down against his hand as he pushed back against her. He rolled his fingers against her jeans, and she had to bite down on something to keep from screaming. His shoulder did the job. Did people get naked in freight elevators? At the rate they were going, would they even make it to naked?

The elevator answered the question for her. It lurched to a stop, breaking all the wonderful tension of the moment and coming way too close to knocking her off the bike—and Ben's hands.

He caught her around the waist before she fell. "We're here," he said with that mischievous smile as he guided her off the bike.

Thank goodness, because between the bike ride and the slow, slow touches, she was so *close* already. Any reservations she might have had about coming home with him were long gone, burned away under the heat of some hard facts. The fact was, she had never physically needed a man so much in her entire life. The fact was, Ben Bolton was more than willing and, she had no doubt, extremely capable. The fact was, she wanted him, and that alone was enough of a reason.

His hand tight around her waist and his body pressed to hers, Ben held her for a second while she checked to see if her legs were up to the task of standing before he let her go and opened the gate. Josey braced herself for the expected onslaught of gray as Ben opened the elevator gate.

He wheeled his bike out, which was weird enough. Who parked in their house?

"Hang on just a second," he said as he rolled off into the darkness. "Let me get the light."

Seconds later, fluorescent lights flickered on over to her left, and Josey found herself next to a full garage. Bright red tool chests—five of them—formed a wall in back, with work benches loaded with all sorts of power tools. Ben rolled his bike to the center of the open space and parked it.

"You live in a garage?"

He gave her a big smile as he closed the distance between them. Her face flushed as he leaned down into her, his lips grazing her temple. "Not quite," he said as he reached behind her and punched some buttons.

One by one, rows of lights flickered on down an aisle that was nearly thirty feet wide. Every fifteen or twenty feet, couches and chairs sat grouped around rugs. White modern chairs sat on a huge black shag rug; chocolate-colored leather sofas crowded Persian rugs. She counted three pseudo-living rooms that stretched back for what looked like a half mile. The space was huge, like measured-not-in-square-feet-but-square-miles huge. She craned her neck upward, searching for a ceiling. Eventually, she was able to see the duct work, but it was maybe twenty feet over her head. The light was bright and airy. Open. Free.

"Whoa." Josey stood in openmouthed shock. This was not what she'd expected. Not even close.

"Come on," Ben said in her ear, causing her to start. For a moment, she'd been so stunned she'd forgotten he was there. She wanted him—oh, how she wanted him—but the magnitude of this place was something else. "Let me show you around."

Before she could be disappointed in this pronouncement, he planted his hand firmly around her waist and guided her to the first seating area, the one with white velvet divans and the shag rug. When they got there, two sets of lights flickered on either side of the aisle.

There was more. Much more.

"You've seen the garage. Then there's my drums and the game room. On the other side in the back is the guest room, then the gym and movie room."

"Oh." Which was not terribly verbose, true, but sounded a heck of a lot better than saying, "You have your own movie room?" She did a slow turn. They weren't rooms, per se, but one area was divided from the next by low walls that looked like they were constructed entirely of glass bricks. The glass caught the overhead lights and reflected brightness around the room. The game room had a TV that looked big enough to be a supporting wall—and the movie room had a similarly huge screen. The main difference was the seating—recliners for the movies, low rockers for the games. A third TV—a smaller one—hung over a rack of free weights, in front of the treadmill.

She spun back to find Ben watching her, his eyes blazing. Without another word, he slid her jacket off her, his fingers brushing against the bare skin on her arms the whole way down. He leaned over her to drop the jacket on one of the sofas—and, in the process, brushed his lips over her neck.

"I like to watch whatever I want, whenever I want," he breathed against her skin. The shiver that ran down her body pushed her into his chest. "Hmm," he hummed against the pulse that was pounding wildly at the base of her neck. But he didn't kiss her, darn it.

Instead, he took her hand and led her toward the next area with the Persian rug. When they got there, the lights behind them shut off and the lights around them turned on. "Pool table and bar," he said, nodding toward the left side as he pushed her down on a leather sofa. His hands stroked her shoulders as he added, "Library and office on the other side."

Had a house tour ever sounded sexier? His voice was low, almost silky, with just a hint of the roughness that made her vibrate with desire.

The pool table and bar were deep mahogany. The lights caught the collection of crystal stemware, making the room gleam with a warmth that invited her to belly up to the bar. The library had a wall of books and another plush, expensive-looking rug underneath a leather recliner that looked comfortably broken in. The office was more Spartan, with just a carved desk and enough technology to run a small corporation in it.

Ben knelt before her, running his hands down over her thighs. This was some sort of torture—he was touching her, making her ache, making her want him more with each featherlight caress—but none of this was him throwing her down and ravishing her. The weight between her legs was painful.

Instead of reaching up and addressing that weight directly, he tugged her boots off her feet. "You seem stunned."

"It's stunning." She'd been in fancy New York apartments with their custom interior decorating jobs and opulent wealth. Heck, her grandparents' apartment hadn't been anything shabby. The stunning thing wasn't so much the opulence—it was that it was *Ben's* opulence.

In New York, this sort of apartment would run the superrich upward of twenty million dollars. Even though they weren't in New York, it still had to have set Ben back at least a couple million. Obviously, his own margins were not nearly so sharp or skinny. *Obviously.*

"I'm glad you like it." He ran his fingers over the now-exposed soles of her feet. What should have flat-out tickled sent shivers of pleasure racing over her. He leaned forward and kissed the top of her thigh through her jeans. The shudder was harder this time, her body dying to respond to his. But he stopped and pulled her to her feet. She all but sank into the rug.

"Just a few more."

More?

Ben led her to the next living room. This one had an abstract rug and furniture that looked well-loved—like he actually used these. As they neared, the lights behind them flickered off and the next set came on.

"Wow," Josey said. A long table was on her left, with seating for twelve. For the first time, she noticed what was on the wall behind the table. A painting that had to be at least twenty feet long and twelve feet high took up the whole wall. An abstract riot of red ran circles around an off-center yellow sun. "Was that one month's rent?"

"*That* I bought outright." Ben's arms circled her waist. "The smaller pieces are rent." He grabbed the hem of her T-shirt and this time, she didn't stop him. *Don't stop,* she thought. House tour, seduction—it was all one and the same. "The kitchen is next to it, and on the other side is my closet."

She would have felt self-conscious at this combination undressing and tour, but she remembered the way he'd kissed her that first time at the school—after grilling her about salaries and students. Always processing the facts, she thought as he hooked his hands into her waistband and undid the button on her jeans.

He slid his hands down over her panties as he pulled her jeans free. Heat radiated from his palms against her bare legs. "The bathroom is behind the kitchen. The bedroom is on the other side." He followed the jeans down, kissing between her breasts and then down her belly.

Normally, she'd be looking for the bedroom, because they'd need a bed. But in this place? It was no understatement to say that he literally had fifty different places that would do just fine.

She stepped free of the pants. Thank heavens she'd had the foresight to wear the matching bra and panties, and that the matching was of a black lace sort. Black lace seemed appropriate to her surroundings.

Ben stood, leaving a trail of heat up her backside as his chest warmed her front. "Obviously beautiful," he said, and she heard the way his voice shook. Then he kissed her as he pulled her hips against his.

From a primal part of her brain, she crowed in victory. He could act all cool and collected, stripping her nearly bare while he showed off the industrial palace he called home, but no man could emerge unscathed from the full impact of black lace.

The tour was done, as of *now*. She pushed him back, reveling in the power she suddenly had over this man. Or maybe not so suddenly, she realized. Maybe now, he was just giving up his control. He was giving it to her.

"Bedroom, you say?" She trailed one finger down his chest, hooking it into his belt just above his throbbing erection. Another shudder went through her as a warm wetness rushed to that spot between her legs. She worked his belt out of the first loop and slipped it free of the buckle.

His eyes drifted shut, and he sucked in a hard breath. "Yeah. The bedroom."

"Do you have…" Condoms could suck the romance right out of a room, but she'd promised to be safe. So this was her, being safe. While she began to unbutton his jeans.

"Several." He grabbed her hands and moved them away from his pants. So maybe he wasn't giving up all of his control.

How nice was it to *not* have to argue or plead or cajole

about condoms? To be with a man smart enough to know they were non-negotiable?

Things were about to get interesting.

He led her farther back. The lights behind them shut off as one small light came on behind a full wall of glass bricks that completely hid the bed from the rest of the wide-open spaces. The glass curved back toward the end of the space, which was a wall of windows that reached from floor to ceiling.

A bed the size of a small country sat in the middle of the room—for this truly was a room—with another abstract painting in softer greens and blues hanging overhead. The sheets were a pristine white with hospital corners so perfectly crisp that she was afraid to mess them up.

Still holding her hand, Ben stepped around the far side of the bed. An old-fashioned reading lamp stood on a table next to the bed. He let go of her to open one of the drawers and pull out a box of condoms—ribbed for her pleasure, she saw. Of course Ben would have planned ahead.

Condoms, check. Bed, check. Desirable, gorgeous man, double check.

Things were about to get *very* interesting.

Josey's hands shook as she peeled off his T-shirt. Finally, she was going to see what all those muscles looked like.

Her breath faltered as she revealed the true magnitude of the body that man was packing underneath his clothing. He was *chiseled.* She'd known his biceps were a sight to behold—all that drumming—but his chest? She had to touch it. He had a small thatch of glossy black hair between pecs of steel. Her fingers traced the six-pack of his abs all the way down to the V of his waist as it cut down hard under his briefs.

He sucked in another breath when she ran her fingers under the fabric. When she ran into something soft yet very, very hard, he grabbed at her again. "Whoa, whoa. I thought you wanted to take it slow." The strain in his voice was un-mistakable. Ben Bolton was a man just barely hanging on to his self-control.

"I never said that." She gave him a shove, sending him back into the bed. "Maybe I don't want it slow." She grabbed hold of his briefs and yanked them off. "Maybe I want it a little rough, a little gritty."

The word *gritty* died on her tongue as he sprang free from the last of his clothes. He was huge. Well, all of him was huge—this part was to perfect scale.

She didn't have long to gawk. Ben sat up with a sicken-ingly easy grace and snatched her hands, pulling her down onto the bed as he rolled over. Before she knew it, she was pinned underneath a naked, aroused man. All that hugeness hung heavy against her leg as he nuzzled her neck.

"My place, my rules. And the first rule is, ladies first. I want this to be memorable."

As he kissed down her neck, Ben let go of her hands and moved lower. Oh, yes, she wanted a memory. But not just one.

No, she didn't just want this night in this bed.

She wanted more.

The clasp on the front of her bra gave, and cold air rushed to beat Ben's hot mouth. He hovered above her for a cool second before he rasped his tongue over her nipple. The total shock of the sensation didn't have time to fully regis-ter before he lowered his whole mouth onto her and fiercely sucked at her flesh. The exquisite pleasure cut through her moodiness. Her hips bucked, but he used his full weight to push her back down to the bed.

"Slow down, woman," he said as he kissed the space be-tween her breasts. "We've got all night."

She tried to say something, but he latched onto her other breast at the same time he nudged her legs apart with his knees. Then that hugeness was pulsing against her black lace, and Josey officially stopped caring about more or less. She just needed to let go of the climax that had been building all night. Heck, if she was being honest, it had been building since she'd first seen Ben Bolton fill a doorway.

That's all she wanted right now. She needed to be filled.

Lucky for her, Ben was up to the task.

"I like these," he murmured against her belly, his hands slipping underneath her panties to cup her backside and pull her legs farther apart. "You're beautiful in them."

"I wore them for you," she managed to say in between gasps.

Ben's mouth moved lower and lower. He nipped at her thigh and traced a path to where she'd neatly trimmed her bikini line. He paused, and Josey found herself wishing she'd gotten a Brazilian. Ben was probably used to girls who were waxed bare, but she didn't have the time, money or pain threshold to do that—man or no man.

As this panicked thought started to whirl around her head, Ben hummed, a noise that sounded suspiciously like satisfaction. "So beautiful," he said as he parted her and ran his tongue—slowly—over her very center.

She let out a cry as he licked her.

Beautiful.

Here, with him, she felt beautiful in a way that had nothing to do with bikini lines or lace panties, but had everything to do with the way he made her feel. Like she was someone special to him. Someone more.

Her body rocked against his, but he wrapped his arms around her legs and held her open as he licked and sucked and kissed harder and harder. Their bodies fell into a rhythm. There was nothing for Josey to do but find something to hold on to and enjoy the ride. She buried her hands in his hair and held on tight.

Higher and higher she flew, until there was nothing left in her world except the pulsing point of contact between her flesh and his. With expert skill, he pushed her past anything she'd ever experienced before until her whole body pulsed with an exploding tightness and she cried out. Even as the climax unleashed its full force upon her, he swept his tongue over her, refusing to let her go numb and weak.

"*So* beautiful," she heard him say as he sat back on his heels and wiped his face. She knew she should say something, but nothing came out. Not even his name.

If he was offended, he didn't show it. Instead, with one corner of his mouth ever-so-slightly curved up, he leaned over and grabbed the condoms off the side table. There was nothing slow about the way he ripped the wrapper open, or the way he rolled it on. But the moment he was sheathed, he took his sweet time kissing his way back up to her lips. All his hugeness pulsed against where she was wetter than she'd ever been before.

"Tell me if I'm going too fast for you," he breathed, his lips just barely touching hers. His voice was low and husky.

"Just right."

He pulled back a little and ran a finger over her slick opening before fitting himself to her. "*You're* just right."

She braced herself for the pain of losing her virginity all over again, but it didn't happen. Ben eased into her at a gentle pace, and Josey was amazed to feel her body take him in without so much as a whimper. All she felt was the sensual joy of his body joining hers. The way he filled her was breathtaking in its satisfaction.

"Josey," he whispered against her neck, and it felt like a prayer.

Then he began to move. Back and forth, he rocked into her. She took everything he gave her and came back for more. And more. And more. Their bodies found that rhythm again, but faster and faster this time, until they'd left "slow" in the dust.

This time, when the world exploded around her, she cried out his name when she came.

With a guttural noise of satisfaction, Ben thrust harder and harder. Still vibrating through the climax, Josey couldn't do anything but hold on to him. He drove deep and groaned as a third, smaller climax hummed through her body. Ben collapsed onto her, making it hard to breathe, but she didn't care.

She'd never felt so whole in her entire life.

He kissed her neck as he pulled out, but he didn't roll off her. "We fit," he said, sounding a little amazed.

She couldn't help but smile. *Fit* wasn't a big-enough word to describe how their bodies had become one—how he'd taken his time to make sure she'd been ready for him. To heck with not being able to breathe. She wrapped her arms around his back and held him tight.

"We do."

She felt his lips curve against her skin before he lifted himself free of her. "I'll get the lights," he said as rolled out of bed and walked out of the room.

Wow. How did he get a butt that fine? Was it the weights, the treadmill—or the motorcycle?

Alone, Josey scooted back until she found some pillows. On the other side, lights flickered on. She could just make out Ben's dark shape, but the particulars were sadly lost to the glass wall's distortion. She pulled the sheet around her, her head swimming and her body tingling. He'd driven her here, but she hadn't been presumptuous enough to pack a change of clothes.

Now what?

Eight

Ben pulled an extra set of towels out of the cabinet and sat them out the counter. Women liked fresh towels, he'd learned. And…yes, a forgotten robe hung on the back of the door. He used it only in the winter, when the drafts created an indoor wind chill. He didn't want her to put her clothes back on, because that meant she'd want to leave, and he wasn't ready to let her go yet. That alone was weird. He hadn't brought a woman back here in a while, and it had been even longer since he'd been with one who looked half as good after as she did before.

The way her body had taken him in was something, but it had taken every bit of his willpower to go slow enough. One thing was clear—she really didn't screw guys she didn't know.

He made sure the toilet was flushed and no huge globs of toothpaste disgraced the sink before he headed out. Josey was wrapped in the sheet, the perfect combination of sensual and innocent. Her cheeks reddened as her gaze surveyed his territory again. Perfect, he thought. No way was he taking her home tonight. He had to know what she looked like when she woke up in the morning.

"Can I get you anything?" She sat up a little straighter in the bed, taking the sheet with her. "There's towels and a robe in the bathroom," he added, hoping that made it clear that she wasn't going anywhere else tonight.

"Water?" Her voice was a little scratchy, but that didn't stop her eyes from taking a few more laps around his body.

Ben fought the urge to flex, just to see what she'd do.

"One water, coming right up." He turned to head to the kitchen. Behind him, he heard the rustle of sheets. Modesty—in small doses—was attractive in a woman. Did she really want the water, or was she just creating some cover?

Didn't matter, he thought as he opened the bottle of San Pellegrino and poured it into two glasses. He headed back to the bedroom, where he remade the bed while he waited. Minutes passed. What was she doing in there? He glanced back down the aisle—all her clothes were still there. Okay. At least she wasn't intent on bailing.

"Ben? Do you have a comb?"

Ben couldn't help but chuckle to himself. Who brushed their hair before they went to bed? Women, that's who. "Top drawer, left side."

"Thanks."

She had a lot of hair—this was probably going to take a while. Ben climbed into bed to wait. Man, he was exhausted. The clock said 11:56 p.m.—just about his regular bedtime, but he usually laid awake in bed for a while until his brain managed to shut the hell up. Right now, he couldn't even keep his eyes open. Unusually energetic sex could do that to a man.

On the other side of his eyelids, the lights went out. He managed to look up to see Josey—in his robe—taking a long drink from her glass. "This is water?"

"San Pellegrino. The stuff that comes out of the tap here tastes like lead." He yawned and patted the bed beside him. If he hadn't been so freaking tired, he'd be happy she was going to stay. He'd be happier if she took off that robe.

The robe slid off her shoulders. He could see the curve of her arms and waist against the light coming in through the windows—sexy as hell, without giving everything away. "Josey," he said before he knew he was talking. Being as he had no idea what was coming out next, he shut his mouth.

She slipped in beside him, her body curling around his without hesitation. The warm weight of her breasts pressed against his chest. He wrapped an arm around her and pulled her even closer, until he could feel her heartbeat.

"Josey," he said again as he kissed the top of her head.

A few moments passed, and he started to drift. So when she said, "Ben," it jolted him back awake.

"Yeah?"

"Why did you buy all those things for the school?"

The way she said it—quiet, serious and *not* sleepy— forced his brain to click back on. He got the feeling that, if he wasn't careful, he'd walk right into a trap.

He must have taken too long, because she went on, "Was it just to impress me..."

Hell, yeah, he'd wanted to impress her. He wanted to turn her on, sweep her off her feet and make her think he was the best she'd ever had. Any man who didn't put that sort of effort into impressing her wasn't worth a damn in his book.

Her heartbeat had picked up a little speed as her fingers clutched at his chest. "You didn't have to spend all that money just to get to tonight. I would have...anyway. I wanted to."

If he lived to be a hundred and forty, he would never figure out women, because she was making it sound like he'd bought her.

"That's not why."

His words came out a little more pissed than he intended, and she shrank away from him.

Aw, screw it.

He lifted her off the bed. She didn't weigh very much—it was easy to set her on his chest, belly-to-belly, full-body contact. "You want to know why I told you I wouldn't give you any money and then bought you stuff."

Maybe he'd scared her too much, because she didn't answer. She just nodded. At least she didn't scramble down off him. Despite his exhaustion and confusion, she felt good on top of him.

Why. A damn fine question. When he put it like that—why *had* he spent so much of his hard-earned money? He could say it was just to impress her—it wouldn't be a total lie—but it wasn't the whole truth.

He closed his eyes again, and the sight of Josey's face when he'd brought all that stuff swam before him. But that wasn't the only thing there. He saw the way Don Two Eagles's contempt became begrudging respect, how those kids went from terror to excitement—how they'd all looked at him and seen someone important. Someone who mattered.

"My old man is ashamed of me." The bitterness of the words cut at his mouth.

"What?" She managed to sound indignant. He took that as a compliment. "You run a company and have a beautiful home and—"

"I'm not the son he's proud of on a Friday night. I'm a bean-counter brainiac. I'm not anything he wanted me to be."

In the dark, she rested her chin on his chest and looked at him. "But the band—"

"The only time he ever heard me play was the night Bobby sang lead. He could care less about me because I'm not him like Billy is and I'm not Mom like Bobby is. I can't be what he thinks I should be." Lord only knew how much time he'd wasted trying.

"But—"

"Doesn't matter." Which was the truth. Here, with her welcoming body covering his, Dad mattered less than he ever had. "And everyone else? They think I'm an arrogant asshole with a heart of stone who only thinks about the bottom line."

She made a little noise of disbelief, but those were the un-varnished facts. People always expected him to be someone else—dangerous biker, drummer, creative welder, smooth-talker—but he wasn't any of those things. He liked the sim-plicity of numbers. He lived in an old factory with artists who cleaned it for him. He played in a band. He didn't make promises he didn't intend to keep, and he always kept the few he did make.

He was holding a beautiful woman. And she was hold-ing him back.

"So why did you get all that stuff?"

She didn't sound spooked by the question this time, which meant he wasn't as spooked to answer it.

"I guess I wanted to prove to someone that I wasn't any of those things. I wanted to prove it to you."

Funny, that was the truth. He wouldn't have thought about it like that if she hadn't pushed him—but wasn't that one of the things that drew him to her? She expected better of him. And he wanted to be better for her.

"I didn't come home with an arrogant asshole."

His head popped up and he looked at her. Now that his eyes had adjusted to the dark, he could make out her eyes. Had he ever heard her cuss before?

She leaned up until their faces were parallel. "I came

home with a man who lets artists pay their rent in paintings. A man who bought drums for complete strangers so
they wouldn't have to share *just* one. A man smart enough
to run a company and crazy enough to play in a rock band.
A man who makes sure ladies are first. I came home with
a true gentleman."

She kissed him, one of those soft-and-gentle things that
should have made him horny but just left him with a strange
sort of lightness.

"Good night, Ben," she murmured as she slid to his side
and wrapped an arm around his waist.

"My Josey" was all he got out before he drifted, trying
to think of what that strange feeling was.

Happy. That's what it was. He felt happy.

Ben woke up at his normal time, with the light stream-
ing in through the windows. He turned to where Josey was
stretched out on her stomach next to him. The sheet was
slung low over her hips and most of her hair was off to one
side, leaving the smooth expanse of her back uncovered.
It had been a long time—way too long—since he'd woken
up wanting a woman. He leaned over and brushed a strand
of hair away from her cheek. He should let her sleep. That
would be the gentlemanly thing to do—and she seemed to
think he was a gentleman.

But he wasn't.

He trailed his fingertips up her back, watching as each
muscle twitched in involuntary response. When he did it a
second time, her eyes fluttered open.

"Hi." Her voice was soft and breathy as she reached over
and touched his cheek.

He went from half-hard to rock-hard in seconds. He should
let her wake up a little, he tried to tell himself. He wasn't
some sex-starved teenager who couldn't control himself.

But something about this woman made him do impulsive, crazy things. He caught hold of her fingers before she could pull them back and kissed her palm. She gasped, her eyes going wide. Then she exhaled, a coy smile on her face.

That was all the invitation he needed. He rolled, pulling her with him until she was right where she'd been last night—on top of him.

She stretched out like a cat after a delicious nap, making the sheet fall away. Yeah, he'd sort of seen those breasts last night, but the difference between light and dark was literally day and night. Her nipples were a deep wine color that almost perfectly matched her lips. This time, he wasn't stopping at just a taste.

He leaned up enough that he could capture one of those perfect breasts. She ground her hips down on him, enough that he could feel her warmth against his erection. When he fastened onto her, a small groan shuddered out of her.

Logically, he knew he should slow down. He should take his time to savor her, make sure that she was ready for him. But the way she moved on top of him—where were the condoms?

He used the last of his self-control to lift her bottom off him and lunge for the nightstand. He snagged a condom on the second try. Quick enough, he got it rolled on and she settled her weight back on him.

"Go slow," he pleaded as her wetness sheathed him. "I want to watch you."

Her eyes drifted shut as she nodded. She had complete control this time, and he was dying to see what she would do with it. She rocked down onto him with great care, making small gasps as she took him in.

The going was slower this time. That was his own greedy fault, but he watched her face for any sign that it wasn't working. None. Her mouth parted as she panted until she surrounded him completely. Once there, she paused to stretch back, giving him plenty of time to feel her firm breasts, her firm backside.

She'd be the death of him, because he'd die for this kind of pleasure. Something about the way she arched her back, the way her small movements felt huge—the way her tightness felt so damn good around him—was different than anything he'd ever felt before.

"You're so beautiful." It was a pitifully inadequate statement of what was blindingly obvious. But it was all his brain could come up with right now.

He forced himself to pay attention when all he wanted to do was let go. She bit that lower lip when something felt extra good. She liked it when he tweaked her nipples with just a little pressure. And when she came? Ah, she shuddered to a stop and then fell forward onto him, her chest heaving. Her body clenched down on his until he had no choice but to give himself up to her.

She fit, like she was made for him.

She leaned back and kissed him as she slid off. "Good morning," she said with a smile that was a little less sleepy, a little more coy.

"Just good? I'll try harder next time."

She grinned at him.

Man, what he wouldn't give to spend the day lounging around with her, but it was Thursday. He'd already had more fun in half an hour than he normally had for the whole day. "When can I see you again?"

The way her cheeks colored that dusty pink—so freaking beautiful. "I have some meetings today, and tomorrow I have to go out to the rez."

"What about tomorrow night? I have band practice after work, but nothing after that. You could come over." Something in her eyes dimmed, and he realized he hadn't asked the right question. "For dinner," he added.

"You cook?" She looked amused—and interested.

"I'll come up with something." Which sounded better than, "Gina makes most of my food." Friday was the day Gina and Pat normally came up to clean. An extra-special dinner wouldn't be too difficult a stretch for the two of them. "We could watch a movie or something." Or have sex again. Maybe even both.

The coffeepot beeped from the kitchen. Damn. It was already six-forty-five and he hadn't showered yet. "I have to go to work," he said with another quick kiss as he got out of bed. "Where do you want me to take you?"

"I don't think the Dean of the College of Education would appreciate me showing up for our accreditation meeting wearing a motorcycle jacket," she said with a sparkling grin. "I need to go home."

"But you'll come back?"

"Yes," she said, getting out of bed and taking his sheet with her. "I'd like that."

By the time Ben left her on the curb outside her apartment with a kiss, a promise to see her tomorrow night and a complicated set of instructions on where to park and how to operate the freight elevator, Josey had less than an hour to shower and get to the university.

On her way there, she called her mother to tell her she'd be back out to the school late Saturday afternoon and all day Sunday. "Oh, Ben Bolton might be coming by on Sunday afternoon," she added as a carefully calculated afterthought.

Mom didn't say anything for a moment. "Did you have fun?"

Fun made it sound like they'd been playing video games

all night instead of having some of the hottest sex she'd ever had the joy of being a part of. "Yeah, Mom. He's nice."

Actually, he was incredibly complicated—she still couldn't get her head around the magnitude of his "place"—but *nice* would have to do.

She had about a million questions for him—starting with why he lived in the old factory and ending with his family. When he'd dropped her off, he'd hinted about wanting to see her place, but she was too embarrassed by the postage-stamp-sized studio she called home to invite him up for a tour.

And if she was embarrassed by her apartment, how would she handle Ben seeing her mom's house? He was a man used to the finest things in life—things that Josey did not have.

Doubt began to set in. True, both of their worlds were in South Dakota. That was more than she'd had with Matt. But the similarities ended there. He was so different from her. Sure, he made nice at the school and at the powwow—but how long would that last? How long before he began to look at her like Matt had, not even trying to hide the contempt?

Worse, how long would it be before the tribe stopped being so welcoming? How long before the whispers started, the same ones people still spread about Grandma? How long before the tribe stopped appreciating the gifts, stopped making nice for the sake of politeness and stopped even looking at Ben? How long before he became the invisible, unacknowledged white man?

But this wasn't about Ben, not really.

Matt had never come to the rez, never met the tribe. Only a few people—Mom, Jenny—had even seen his picture or known how badly he'd broken her heart. Everyone—the whole damned tribe—knew about Ben. How long before she became the traitor to the tribe? Before people like Don Two Eagles forgot about all the work she'd done to get the school going, to take care of her people? How long before *she* became the invisible, wannabe white woman?

Don't be ridiculous, she thought. If there was one undeniable fact that she had to remember, it was that the only things Ben and Matt had in common were maleness and whiteness. And yes, people would talk. But their gossip didn't define her. She knew what she wanted. Rather than get stuck trying to game plan a response to every individual criticism of her life, she needed to focus on the here and now.

Ben was nice. Dinner sounded promising. As much as she already couldn't wait to see what other bedroom tricks that man had up his sleeve, she wanted to understand him. She hoped he wanted to understand her.

The sex had been memorable. *Unforgettable.*

But she wanted more.

Nine

Josey parked in a spot marked *Reserved* beside the factory next to the van that she thought belonged to the guy named Stick. The moment she opened her car door, the sound of caterwauling filled the air. She was early. The band was still here.

She grabbed her overnight bag and locked her doors. She debated heading toward the noise—she did like to watch Ben play, after all—but then she remembered the crude comments the other two band members had made. Maybe she'd just go upstairs.

The freight elevator seemed even spookier this time, but she figured out where the hidden keypad was and got the code right on the second try. Her stomach was doing wonderfully conflicting flips as the thing lurched its way up. She didn't want to admit to herself how much she'd been looking forward to another night with Ben—and how excited she'd been about spending a little more time at his place. But to just walk right in, like she owned it? At best, this was a third date, assuming the first three meetings counted as one total outing. She was prepared this time, with a little lube she'd snagged at the drugstore and her own toothbrush. She should feel ready. But she didn't.

She belonged in this world, she reminded herself. She fit here. She fit on the rez, too. It was fine to walk in both worlds. And besides, it wasn't like the whole of the tribe was sitting around Ben's apartment, watching them like old-fashioned chaperones, ready to smack Ben's knuckles with a ruler if he so much as looked at her funny. This relationship was no one else's business except hers and Ben's. That's all there was to it.

Finally, the elevator came to a jarring stop, sending her stumbling. That darn thing was going to take a lot of getting used to. She got the door open and heard—music? Wasn't Ben down with the band?

Fighting a rising tide of dread, she stepped out into the apartment. "Hello?" she called, but the pounding piano drowned her out. No one was in the band area—she didn't see anyone at all. A lilting woman's voice echoed around her. Did Ben even like Sarah McLachlan?

She walked down the main aisle. Without Ben in it, this place gave her the creeps. It was too big, too empty—all the furniture notwithstanding. How did he stand it here all by himself?

Unless he wasn't all by himself. She realized it was brighter up front, near the kitchen. Someone was here.

"Hello? Ben?"

A head—a female head—popped out from behind a cabinet. "Oh, hey! You're early!"

Josey froze. "Excuse me?"

The woman—with fire-engine-red hair and piercings in her nose, ears and eyebrows—clicked a remote. The music faded away as she came around the island and gave Josey an explicit once-over. "Wow. He said you were beautiful, but *damn,* girl. Look at you!" She let out a wolf whistle and then called out over Josey's shoulder, "Baby! Come meet the new girl!"

"Um, what?" Josey's head began to spin. She'd thought— Ben had acted like— What kind of stuff was he *into?*

Footsteps echoed behind her. Josey spun awkwardly to see another punk-ish girl striding toward her, except this one had artificially black hair and far too much eyeliner. She advanced on Josey with a predatory stare. "Not what I was expecting," she said in a quiet voice.

That would make two—or possibly three, Josey couldn't tell—of them. These women acted like they knew her—like they knew Ben.

"So, you and Ben, huh?" The black-haired one circled around Josey on her way to join the redhead. Before Josey could answer the not-quite-a-question, the black-haired one slipped an arm around the redhead's waist and kissed her neck without taking her eyes off Josey.

Josey made a snap decision that she needed to be as brazen as these women clearly were. Otherwise, they might eat her alive. "Yes. Ben and I."

"He likes you," the redhead volunteered, leaning back into the black-haired woman's arms.

She didn't even know how to respond to that. So she went with, "Oh?"

Both women smiled. The redhead's was warm and friendly. The black-haired one's was mercenary. "I've always wanted to know—is he good?"

"Excuse me?" Josey couldn't help it. She took a step back.

"If I had to pick one of the Bolton boys, I'd pick Ben."

"Really?" The redhead turned enough to give the other

one a funny look. "I'd totally do Bobby before Ben. But not Billy. He's a little too scary."

"Of course you'd pick Bobby," the dark one said. "But I like Ben. He's serious, intense. I bet he'd be great in bed. Is he?"

Both women turned expectant gazes back to where Josey was edging away from them.

"Well…" She wasn't one to kiss and tell, and this felt a hell of a lot like telling.

The redhead turned back to her companion. "I'm not disagreeing with you. But Bobby—he'd be all over a ménage à trois. If I were going to sleep with a man, I'd want you to be there with me. And Bobby would *totally* get off watching us go at it, baby. He'd think he'd died and gone to heaven. Ben would never go for that—he'd consider it cheating or something ridiculous. He's a one-woman kind of man."

"Oh, honey, that's so sweet of you." The black-haired woman kissed the redhead—on the mouth!—and although Josey was trying not to look, she was pretty sure the redhead was giving as good as she got.

This situation was so far out of her control as to be laughable. Bailing was the only sane option. Girl-on-girl—with or without a Bolton watching—was not part of her plans for the evening. Or her life. She took another step backward—and ran into something hard and warm and slightly damp.

Long arms circled around her waist, and light stubble scratched at her ear. "You made it," Ben said, pulling her back into his chest. "Did you meet the girls? Oh." He sighed in frustration. "Hey, knock it off!" he thundered, right in her ear. "Sorry."

"Oops." The redhead giggled. "Our bad, boss."

Boss? What the heck?

"So you've met the girls?"

Both of the "girls" shot her a smarmy smile. Met? No. Been menaced by? Yes. "Only just."

"Josey White Plume, this is Gina Cobbler," he said, indicating the redhead, "and Patrice Harmon. They're the artists-slash-maids I was telling you about."

"You *seriously* forgot gourmet chef?" Gina rolled her eyes. "Men."

The artists. Slash maids. And chef. The overwhelming relief that these women weren't manifestations of Ben's kinky side but merely eccentric employees made Josey's knees knock together.

"You okay?" Ben whispered in her ear as his arm tightened around her waist a little more.

"I think so." Better than she'd been ten minutes ago. The artists—she'd assumed it was a man and woman. Not two women.

Who'd never slept with Ben. Who believed he was a one-woman man.

"Good. Will you be okay for a few minutes? I've got to shower."

"We'll be fine," Gina told him. "Go, before you stink up the joint. We'll give her the tour."

Ben came around to kiss her on the lips before he headed for the glassed-off bathroom. "I already gave her a tour," he shouted back over her shoulder. He peeled off his shirt and dropped it on a sofa.

"Men," Gina repeated. "He probably told you the obvious—he's got a gym and a movie room and a kitchen, that sort of thing." She spun around to peek in on something in the oven.

"Well, yes," Josey admitted, taking a cautious jump back into the conversation. She still wasn't sure about Patrice, but Gina seemed mostly friendly. "There's more?"

"If you're going to spend any time here—which we're *all*

assuming you are, as he's already given you the key codes—you need to have the *real* tour."

Getting the key codes was a big deal?

Josey suddenly realized that Gina—and Patrice—were Ben's personal versions of that receptionist at Crazy Horse. Flattery would get a girl everywhere. "You're right. And dinner smells delicious."

"Thanks!" Gina said brightly. "It's one of Ben's favorites."

In the next fifteen minutes, Josey learned where the cups, forks and plates were; how to turn on both TVs; how to start the treadmill; and which mini-fridge had the red wine and which had the white. She learned how to turn the lights on and off and how to change the music. She even learned where the stairway was—"He only uses the elevator when he's on the bike," Gina told her.

She heard about how "the girls," as they collectively referred to themselves, had met Ben about four years ago at a gallery showing he'd attended with a date.

"First and last time we ever saw that one," Gina said in a conspiratorial whisper. "She didn't *appreciate* art. You do something with a school, right? Don't tell her I told you, but Patrice *loves* kids. Quiet ones, anyway. Sometimes, we pack our stuff up and hang out in the cancer ward. Those kids *appreciate* art. Maybe we could come out to your school? That would be cool. Ben didn't say if you had an art teacher or not, but everyone should throw paint at a canvas at *some* point in their lives, don't you think?"

Josey could only nod along. Gina talked *fast*. As she shot off ideas and plans at tommy-gun speed, Patrice disappeared into a back room again, carrying Ben's discarded shirt. "Laundry," Gina informed her. "Ben doesn't 'do' laundry, but if you need to, it's back there. Otherwise, Patrice does it when we're here."

"And how often are you here?"

"Every other week." Gina hurried back to the kitchen when a timer went off. "He'll cook eggs and stuff, but I make dinners he can reheat whenever he gets home and we keep the place clean. He doesn't charge us much rent at all and doesn't care who crashes. We've got plenty of studio space and no nosy neighbors. As long as we don't set the joint on fire or do anything illegal, we can stay. We *love* it here." She turned a surprisingly stern glare to Josey. "He's a nice guy, although he doesn't want *anyone* to know it. Don't jerk him around."

Josey bristled under the implication. "I wasn't planning on it."

"Good." The moment passed, and Gina was off again. She told Josey all about how Ben had let them decorate this place. "When we got here, it was still *so* a factory. He had a big bed in the corner, but it was awful. All gray. *Terrible.*"

Like his office. Josey looked at Gina and smiled. "Men and color, huh?"

"Totally," was the answer she got before Gina was telling Josey how Ben held formal parties for people wearing tuxedos and leathers every so often, and how Gina would make the craziest appetizers she could think of while Patrice and whatever buddies they could gather up walked around with serving trays.

"We met Brad Pitt—pre-break-up. He'd ordered a bike and wanted to come pick it up himself. And Pink—she was so *nice!*—and even Jack Nicholson."

"Anarchy," Patrice called out from somewhere.

"Oh, yeah! The whole cast of that *Sons of Anarchy* show, too."

Josey couldn't help but be impressed. She was standing where Nicholson and Pitt had stood? "Wow."

Gina nodded enthusiastically. "Ben bitches and moans about Bobby schmoozing, but secretly, he's *just* as bad.

Looks damn fine in a tux, too. If I weren't a lesbian…" She got a wistful look in her eye. "Well, maybe not. It'd be like boinking my *brother,* you know? Ew."

"Um…"

"Did you see the paintings?" Gina appeared to be completely oblivious to the discomfort she slung around. Luckily, Josey's mortification was short-lived. Gina talked too darned fast. "Patrice, she does the abstract stuff. She's *really* good. She had a gallery show in Denver a few months ago."

"Wow." That word seemed appropriate and short enough that Josey could actually get it in edgewise. "How about you?"

"Oh—totally different. I do portraits. Takes me months to get them *just* right. I'm *soooo* slow!" This last bit came out as a wail.

"She did the one over there." Patrice motioned to the library as she walked past Josey with a basket of folded sheets. "It's Ben's favorite."

Gina blew a kiss after her. "You're *so* sweet!"

Oh, dear. Josey decided that the best course of action was to go look at the painting before those two got all lovey-dovey again.

The portrait was about the size of a sheet of paper, so it blended in with all the books that surrounded it in the middle of the library shelves. As Josey got closer, her first impression was of bright, California sun. The woman pictured had the kind of blond hair that came straight from a beach and a wide smile. The angle of her body made it look like she was sitting at a table or something, smiling up at the viewer. She was young and beautiful.

"It's a lovely portrait," Josey said, trying her darnedest to focus on the artistic merit of the piece and ignore whatever irrational jealousy she felt toward the woman who had earned the right to sit on Ben's shelf.

"It's my mother."

Josey jumped. She'd been so absorbed in the art that she hadn't heard him come up next to her. She glanced at him. Bare feet, wet hair, gray T-shirt and faded blue jeans. How could he possibly look any better in a tux than he did right now?

"She's lovely." Josey studied the face. "You have her eyes."

Ben wrapped her up in a hug. She loved how she fit with him, how his chin rested on her forehead, how his arms seemed to belong around her waist. When he was near, what seemed big and spooky about his apartment suddenly felt cozy and just right.

"Bobby looks more like her than I do." He sounded resigned to the sibling rivalry.

"Dinner's on the table! Byeeeee!" At the far end, a door clicked shut.

They were alone. Ben spun her around and kissed her.

"So," she said, clearing her throat and trying to grasp everything that had happened in the past half hour. She wasn't sure she was doing a very good job of it.

"So," he agreed. For a moment, they stood there, arms around each other. It was a simple hug—the earth did not move and choirs did not sing—but Josey couldn't help but feel a connection with Ben that she'd never felt with anyone before. Not even in bed.

"We should eat before it gets cold." He took her hand and led her away from the kind eyes of his mother.

Dinner was indeed on the table. Twice-baked potatoes, spring greens, a homemade loaf of bread and something that looked like a cross between a roast and a Hostess Ho Ho. A bottle of red wine—a shiraz—was breathing on the table. The smells that had been lurking around the apartment hit Josey full-on. The crystal wine goblets caught the light of the taper candles and threw a warm glow around them. "You have a chef." It was almost too much.

"Gina watches a lot of cooking shows. This is braciola, I think. It's good." He sliced the bread and then the meat. "How was the meeting at the university?"

Josey didn't bother to hide her grin. He wasn't asking it because he felt he was obligated. She could tell by the way that he watched her that he was actually interested. "Good."

In between bites of some of the best—and flattest—steak she'd ever had, she told him that, because all of her supply problems had disappeared, she was now working on getting the program certified by the state.

He finished chewing and notched an eyebrow at her. "Let me guess. Don is the sticking point?"

The level of attention he paid to her was making her warm. "He's provisionally certified. He has a year to complete several classes on child development. A fact that he has yet to learn." And she wasn't exactly looking forward to telling him.

"You should sell tickets to that conversation—like a fundraiser for the school. I'd buy one."

"Don't think I haven't thought about it." Ben regarded her with open curiosity. The room's temperature seemed to go up another notch under the heat of that gaze. "What?"

"Are you certified?"

"No. I'm not a teacher."

"You're a corporate fundraiser. Except I don't know what corporation needs to hold fundraisers." He turned his attention back to the braciola, making it seem like a casual question.

Josey knew better. Wine or no wine, she could tell when someone was fishing for information. "Depends on how you define *corporate*. Most hospitals are corporations, and a good many universities operate like one. I started out at the New York University Hospital. My grandfather was on the board."

He didn't say anything for a moment. She could see him thinking, and she wondered which way he'd go—how she got here from NYU, or... "The same grandfather who left you in charge of a trust fund?"

"The very same."

His smile was cryptic. "You don't act anything like the trust-fund babies I've met before."

"You've met other trust-fund babies with a last name like White Plume?"

"Point taken."

Josey topped off her wineglass. How many trust-fund babies *did* he know? "My great-grandfather Harold Stewart was a banker. He ran things for J. P. Morgan, II." She pointed to her head. "That's where the red hair came from."

"Impressive."

"I don't know if you know this, but Morgan Sr. fronted the money for Edward Curtis to take all those famous photos of American Indians. And Harold idolized the Morgans. So he took it upon himself to do a little documenting. He packed up my grandfather, George, and lit out for the Plains in a Cadillac."

"I've heard of Curtis."

He waited for her to go on. A man who listened, she marveled. How rare was that?

"They got a flat tire forty miles from Wall, South Dakota. A Lakota named Samuel Respects None found them."

"How old was George?"

"Ten. They spent the whole summer vacation with Samuel. Harold bought anything—ancient artifacts, new dance costumes—he could get his hands on. He spread more money around the rez than most people had seen in their lifetimes." Harold had been an outsider, and he'd bought the respect of the tribe. Josey wondered if Ben was doing the same. Some days, she wondered if, with her trust fund, that's what she was doing, too.

"So Sam invited him back?"

"Every summer for the rest of his life. They were family. When Harold died in 1952, Sam even made the trip to New York for the funeral." She smiled. This was the part of the story she liked. "He brought his granddaughter, Mary, with him. She stayed."

It had always seemed like such a romantic tale—two starcrossed lovers from different worlds finding a way to be together, no matter what the cost. She looked at Ben. Is this connection what Grandma had to go all the way to New York to find?

"So Samuel Respects None's granddaughter was your grandmother? The one from the bluff?"

"And Mom was their only child. He loved my grandmother very much." That one truth—the truth that no one could ever deny or take away—was the thing that made Josey hold her head high when people looked at her sideways.

Grandpa and Grandma had loved deeply and passionately until their last days on this earth. The dementia that took her grandmother away from Josey, then her mother, couldn't touch her love of George Stewart. Even when Grandma couldn't recognize her husband as an old man, she would sit with photos of him from his first visit to the rez, when he had been ten and Grandma had been six, and tell Josey in an awestruck whisper, "I like this boy. I'm going to marry him." And Josey would pat her hand and assure her that, yes, she would, and they'd live happily ever after.

Sheesh. One or two glasses of wine, and she was getting misty-eyed. Reading too much into Ben's attentiveness was a recipe for disaster. She sniffed and tried to pull herself together.

Ben gave her a minute to get things under control before he blissfully steered the conversation away from loves-of-a-lifetime. "He wanted to make things better."

"His father had paid for Grandma to go to a private school off the rez when she was young. He had a provision in his will that paid for her college in New York, too. When she died, Grandpa tried to think of the best way he could honor her memory. So Mom and I got enough to live on, but the rest of the money went toward building the school."

"Warren Buffet would have been proud."

Josey broke out in a laugh. "Actually, they didn't get along. Grandpa preferred Pepsi."

Ben laughed with her, a rich, full sound that warmed her even further. So it probably was the wine, but really—how many men could she sit down to dinner with who would make jokes about Warren Buffet? Who'd also heard of Curtis and not one, but two J. P. Morgans? And—this was the kicker—who *didn't* laugh at names like White Plume and Respects None?

Very few. She'd be hard-pressed to come up with another.

The remains of dinner sat on the table. Ben stood and began to gather the dishes. "So, Gina talked your ear off?"

"Both of them." She handed him the dishes, he rinsed them under the tap and put them in the dishwasher. Despite having hired help, he seemed comfortable fending for himself.

Ben laughed again. "At least she doesn't have access to any of my baby pictures." He shut the dishwasher and, leaning back on the counter, gave her a look that she couldn't quite read. "Do you know how to play pool?"

Ten

Josey stood next to the table, leaning against her stick and swaying to the John Legend music Ben had put on. The way her hips were moving was enough to distract him from the game. Too bad she didn't seem to notice she was doing it.

"You play a lot of pool?"

"When I have someone to play with. Stick used to come up after practice, but he's got a girlfriend now. Bobby likes to play for money, but he's kind of a jerk about it." Ben sank the striped fourteen. He didn't have to ask if she played a lot. She'd gotten two balls in. He had one to go. "Billy will play, if I can get him out of the shop. But that's a big if."

"Can I ask you a question?"

He lined up the shot. "You don't need my permission. Ask away."

"Why do you live in the old shop? And why is it so much bigger than the new one?"

He took an extra second to make the shot. On to the eight ball. "I grew up here. It just felt like home."

"Really?" She didn't seem to mind in the least that he was about to beat her.

"Yeah. Back when Crazy Horse was Dad's business, he didn't do custom stuff. He had models, and he had guys who built them assembly-style. He made more bikes, so he had to store more bikes. Mom handled the books then. We'd all get up early and come here, then Mom would take us to school and bring us back here afterward. Some nights we'd be here until late, but Mom liked to keep the family together, she always said."

Keep the family together. That had been what he'd promised her.

"That must have been hard."

"It wasn't so bad. As long as we didn't break anything, we pretty much got to roam free. We built forts out of boxes and had gear wars—like ninja stars, but with gears."

She gave him a look of amused disbelief. "You threw gears at each other?"

"Hey, I only chipped Bobby's tooth that one time."

His innocent look didn't work—of course, it hadn't worked on Mom, either. Josey's mouth dropped open in shock, which gave him all sorts of ideas. Instead, he sank the eight ball and began to rerack the balls. Now that he thought about it, it had been a long time since he'd played pool with anyone. Even if she wasn't very good at it, it was still nice to play with her and have a real conversation.

"Okay." The way she said it made it clear that it wasn't, really, but she didn't harp on it. "So the new factory..."

"Billy didn't—doesn't—like mass-produced anything. He convinced Dad he could make more money doing one custom bike at a time than doing one hundred cookie cutters. He got Bobby to back him up, and I ran the numbers. Dad will argue with one or two of us, but he figured all three Boltons agreeing on something was as close to a sure thing as he was going to get. So we switched. Two years later, we had made enough to build the shop. That was almost six years ago."

"I see." She looked around. "I like what you've done with the place."

"I'm sure Gina told you she did most of it."

"Maybe." She let out a soft giggle and bent over to break. It would be poor sportsmanship to run his hands over the swell of her bottom while she was shooting. He settled for staring.

"You think it's pretentious to have resident artist-maids."

This shot was better. Two stripes actually went in as the balls careened around the table. She almost looked like she knew what she was doing. "Don't forget chef."

"How could I?"

Still bent almost double, she looked back over her shoulder. "Any other surprises? You're not hiding mimes in the basement or anything?"

"No mimes." Sweet merciful heavens, she was still swaying. Her bottom was in serious danger of hypnotizing him. "You?"

"Nothing like Gina. Hang on."

In six consecutive shots, she cleared the table. He stood gaping at her as the eight ball went down without a whimper. "You let me win?"

"Of course not." Her innocent look was much more effective than his would ever be. "I was getting a feel for how you play the game."

She'd let him win to make sure he'd lose. She could give as good as she got. Man, what a woman.

She set down her cue. "I'm about done playing for tonight." She put her hands on his cheeks and pulled him into her until her lips scorched his. The idling erection he'd been trying to ignore went full throttle in a heartbeat. When she pulled away from him, she licked her lips and breathed, "You?"

"Finished." His cue clattered to the ground and he actually swept her off her feet. There was a first for everything.

For the first time, the size of his place bugged him. Between dancing around the furniture and kissing Josey, it took forever to get back to the bed. She was wearing a red bra with a matching pair of panties that sat low on her hips and begged a man to peel them off. He was willing—more than willing—to put the time and energy into a right and proper seduction, but when he had her nude before him, her body already wet for him, he barely got the condom on before he took what she so willingly gave him.

She rose to meet him again and again. She dug her nails into his back—not enough to draw blood, but enough that the sensation spurred him on. She felt so damn good. Everything about her was good. His name sounded just right coming out of her mouth as a moan. Her legs fit just so around his waist. He tried to go slow, but he couldn't hold back. Not with her. Something about her…

After she'd gotten cleaned up and they'd wrapped themselves around each other in bed, Ben said, "I like this."

"Just 'like'? I'll try harder next time," she said with a sleepy yawn. Underneath the covers, she stretched out her legs and stroked his ankle with her toes.

"Not just that—all of this. Dinner, pool—and *that*. I like it all. I like you."

She got very still before taking a careful breath. "I like you, too."

There it was again—that strange feeling. This happiness thing was getting out of hand.

Ben was getting used to it.

* * *

"Well, well, well." Jenny launched a paint roller at Josey's head. "Look who's back."

Josey threw the roller back. "It's been, what? Three days? I don't consider that 'gone.'"

Jenny was like a bulldog. Once she latched onto an idea, she wouldn't let go of it until it was good and dead. "So, how is he?"

Josey did a quick check, but the two women were alone in the seventh- and eighth-grade room. Everyone else was outside using as many power tools as the generators could support. She could hear Don bellowing instructions through the walls.

The second time in two days someone had asked her that question. And, once again, she had no intention of answering. Instead, she made a play for Jenny's outsize maternal instincts. "Have you talked to Jared recently? He was feeling a little picked on at the powwow."

Jenny let out a short laugh. "Nice try, but you didn't think that would work, did you? You show up at a powwow with Mr. Super Hunk, disappear for three days and expect nobody to put one and one together?"

Oh, heavens, people were talking. Guessing. And, by all estimations, getting close to the truth. The churning anxiety made Josey's stomach turn worse than drinking sour milk. Was it better or worse that she'd run into Jenny first? When she went out to talk to Don later, would he meet her eyes, or would he barely acknowledge her existence?

No. She would not let other people define her. She knew what she wanted, and right now, what she wanted was not to talk about her love life. What she wanted was for everything to be normal. And the one way she knew how to ensure that was to act as normal as she could.

Josey pulled herself up to her full height and looked down

her nose at her cousin. "I expect certain people to mind their own business."

Like she could intimidate Jenny. The woman was a force to be reckoned with. She bounced on the balls of her feet and clapped her hands. "Ooh. Either really bad or really, really good. Does he live in a garage or a palace?"

"If I tell you, can we get to work?" Jenny nodded and made a big show of mixing the paint. "Can you keep it to yourself?" Jenny nodded even more enthusiastically. Luckily, Josey knew her cousin would keep that promise—especially if she ever wanted any more tidbits. "Both. He remodeled the top floor of an old factory and parks his bike in it. How are things coming out there on the shop?"

"Wow, you must like him."

It was a lot to ask for people not to put one and one together. Josey knew this. That didn't make dealing with it any easier. She pushed her anxiety further down, desperately trying to ignore it entirely. She'd worked too hard to make her place in this tribe to let something like a casual relationship with Ben Bolton derail her plans.

Normal, she reminded herself, keeping her tone light. "He's nice. Did you get my message about the certification?"

Jenny whistled and poured the paint. "Three subject changes. I amend my previous statement to 'really like.'"

"Okay, I really like him. Happy?"

Jenny stuck her hands on her hips, tilted her head sideways and stared at her. "You look happy." Josey rolled her eyes, but Jenny didn't let it drop. "You do! I mean, I'd kill for your bone structure, but you always look like you're having to work at a smile. It's like you've got to prove to people that you're thrilled to be here in the middle of nowhere. But today?" Jenny gave her a wistful smile. "Happy."

And that's why Josey loved her cousin. Despite the fact that Jenny was full-blooded Lakota, she was one of the few people on this reservation who never held her mixed heritage against Josey. She always understood.

For the first time since Josey had driven back onto the rez this morning, she felt herself breathe. Not everyone would approve. Not everyone had to. If Jenny and Mom still treated her like the same old Josey-from-the-block, then it didn't much matter what the whole tribe thought. "He gave me the keys—well, the key codes—to his place."

Jenny whistled. "How many nights?"

"Two."

"And he's coming out here tomorrow?"

"Dinner at Mom's. Just as soon as I tell Mom." That part made her a little nervous. Okay, a lot nervous. Although she didn't talk about it too much, Josey was pretty sure that Mom had had her heart broken by a white man back in the day, which was why she'd come back to the rez and married Dad. Josey's last heartbreak had been hard on both of them. She didn't know if Mom would react well to Josey giving another white man a chance to break her heart again.

They fell into an easy silence as they painted the classroom. Jenny did the cutting in while Josey started on the ceiling. The work went much faster than it did when the tasks were divided between ten *helpful* girls. The whole thing was done in less than an hour.

Jenny dropped her brush on the drop cloth and clenched her hands a few times. "Is he perfect?"

Josey thought about his overwhelming need to be in charge, the conflicted feelings he had about his family and—if left to his own devices—his penchant for gray as a go-to color. She giggled. "No. Not even close."

"But he's rich?"

"Yes."

"Handsome?"

"Very."

"And he's footing the bill for more tools?"

"That's the plan." A plan that would take another month or so to come to fruition. Something about that time frame felt cozily long-term.

Jenny sighed, a mix of concern and pity. Then she shot Josey a sneaky grin. "Does he have a brother?"

Not surprisingly, Billy was in the shop at ten on a Saturday morning. He grunted when Ben got within acknowledgment range. "What are you doing here?"

"I work here. How's the trike coming?"

Billy glared at him from underneath bushy eyebrows. "Same woman, or different?"

Ben chose not to answer that. He made a slow circle around the trike. Billy had the engine on the frame. "Looks good."

Billy grunted again. So much for conversation. Just to bug the big man, Ben pulled up a stool and watched him. He was promptly ignored.

As Billy worked, Ben's mind drifted. It started on Josey—more specifically, the way she looked when she woke up, half asleep and half turned on. Man, she'd been all sorts of turned on by that high-speed ride down the highway after dark. He wondered if she'd want to learn to ride. Years had passed since he'd last built a bike from the ground up—if he made one for her, would she ride it? Would she even like it?

He shifted on the stool. Being as he wouldn't get to see her either sleepy or turned on for another couple of days, he forced his mind to move on to less painful thoughts. He saw Billy had some brochures for new—and expensive—equipment on his workbench.

Snatches of conversations from the past few days jumbled together in his head. Grandfathers—white and Indian—lifelong friends—fundraisers. Those concepts didn't mix with that kid—what was his name? The one with the bad hair? Jared? Or the way people kept a buffer zone around Josey's mom. But those other kids—the tough ones—those kids had lost almost all of their attitudes when it came to his bike.

Ben started out of his daze. That was it.

"Billy."

His big brother jumped, dropping a wrench on his boot. "Dammit, what?"

"Would you teach kids how to build a bike?"

"What the hell are you talking about?"

"At Josey's school—the boys want to build a bike. They could sell it for a fundraiser."

"So she has a name."

Ben bristled. He didn't bug Billy about his lady friends and he expected the same courtesy. "You're the one going on and on about Mr. Horton. You're the one who talks about giving respect, instead of having to earn it the hard way."

That was what Horton had done for Billy. He'd never held him to an unattainable standard and then punished him for not reaching it. Maybe Ben could do that for those kids. He might never get his father's respect—but that didn't mean he had to treat everyone else the same way. He could break the cycle. He could make things better.

"I'm talking about paying it forward. But, hey—you don't want to help out kids everyone else has given up on? That's your business." He jumped to his feet and stomped toward the door.

"Now wait just a goddamn minute," Billy roared behind him.

Ben pulled up short, making sure to wipe the victory smile off his face before he turned around. "Yeah?"

Nothing with Billy was easy. He let Ben hang for another

ten minutes while he fiddled around on the trike. "Can't have kids running around the shop."

"They're building a shop at the school. Josey loved the tools you kicked in."

Another long stretch of silence. Finally, Billy said, "Can't build a bike with circ saws."

Grinning his fool head off would make Billy cagey, so Ben picked up the brochure. Whether his big brother knew it or not, he was easy to play.

"Yeah, you're right. I wouldn't be able to find the equipment. That stuff isn't easy to come by."

He sat back down and flipped through the slick marketing copy. The latest in top-of-the-line metal lathes had computerized balancing, accurate to 0.00001 millimeters.

Billy was muttering to himself while Ben moved on to a flyer for a new additive technology printer, which was a machine that could print a part for small businesses. So Ben didn't build like Billy did. Even he could see the immediate value of a machine that could print out a prototype.

A plan was crystallizing in his mind. If there was one thing Billy loved, it was new and improved. On more than one occasion, he had complained about having to use the same heavy equipment that Dad had been using since the Reagan era. Crazy Horse could order some new-and-improved machinery, and then they'd donate the old-and-unimproved stuff to the school—thereby earning hefty tax deductions and the devoted love of Josey White Plume. And everyone else on the rez, but mostly Josey.

The plans took a turn away from modern technology. A vision of her on a small, sleek machine—red, like her hair—speeding down a sunlit highway next to him popped into his mind. He'd never been a flowers-and-chocolates kind of guy, anyway.

Billy cleared his throat and scratched at his beard, bringing Ben back to the here and now. "I was telling Jimbo the other day, this lathe won't stay centered for more than three, maybe four rounds. Still got a lot of life in it, but all the extra recalibrating is a lot of downtime."

No doubt about it, Ben had his big brother right where he wanted him. "Time is money."

Billy trotted out his fierce look. "Don't know about teaching a bunch of kids about building a bike, though."

"Don't worry about that right now. If you *need* some new stuff, you should have some new stuff. Top of the line, like your bikes."

"Yeah." Billy sounded more enthusiastic. "Been wanting to try out a few things, but on this old stuff...too risky, you know?"

"Gonna take some time," Ben added. "Gotta move some money around, lay down some financing." Figure out how to work around Dad. He didn't say it out loud, but Billy met Ben's eyes. Going around Dad instead of through him was the only way, because the old man would never sign off on something as radical as a printer that printed parts.

It would take some serious planning to pull it off, but once the equipment was here and Billy was boosting his productivity, Dad would have to agree that Ben was fully capable of making smart business decisions. Once he got over being left in the dark, that was. It was risky, but it was a risk Ben was willing to take.

"I got time." Billy looked around, a sense of weariness sitting on him like an ill-fitting crown. "All the time in the world." He shook it off and shot Ben an actual smile. "All this talk of building bikes—and you haven't built one in years."

"Actually," Ben said, feeling the truth of it, "I was thinking about starting one."

Billy shook his head, like he just couldn't believe his own eyes. "This Josey must be a piece of work."

Ben didn't bristle this time. He was going to take his victory and run with it.

He had a lot of work to do.

After a weekend of frenzied housekeeping, Josey's mom was ready. Ben showed up Sunday night with a box of chocolates and a small African violet. He said nothing about the shabby double-wide trailer that was home. Instead, he complimented Mom on how much he liked the comfortable couch and how cozy everything was. He studied the picture of Josey's dad, Virgil, and listened intently as Mom talked about his military service.

Over a dinner of fried chicken and baked potatoes, he told them how he'd arranged to donate heavy shop equipment when they bought new computer-based tools, and how he thought it would be a good idea if his older brother, Billy, came out with him after Don got the shop finished and helped the kids build a bike they could auction off for charity.

The more he talked, the wider Mom's eyes got as her gaze darted between Josey and Ben. Soon all she could say was, "That's—why, that's a wonderful idea!"

"They'll need to be able to operate all the tools first, so it probably won't happen this school year," he cautioned, that hidden smile tugging at the corner of his mouth.

Mom shot Josey another stunned look. "You knew about this?"

"I wanted it to be a surprise," Ben said with a sheepish smile that was unnecessarily attractive.

He'd wanted to surprise her, something that required forethought and planning. As Mom and Ben discussed the particulars, a warm, taken-care-of feeling spread throughout Josey. This was such a far cry from Matt's disconnection from anything tribal. That had to make it a good thing, right.

After all, Ben was a problem-solver. He was doing what he did best, she realized.

But that didn't answer the question of what would happen between the two of them when there was no longer a problem to solve. Or when the problem wasn't something he *could* solve.

He could donate tools and instruments and even a bike, but he couldn't make people accept him on anything more than a surface level. He couldn't be a member of the tribe, no matter how generous he was, just like Grandpa had never truly been accepted by anyone other than Samuel Respects None and his granddaughter, Mary. For all his generosity, for all his goodwill, Grandpa had never been accepted. His granddaughter had never been fully accepted, despite a lifetime of trying. Would Josey ever find her place in the tribe, especially if she was involved with another outsider?

That was the problem Ben Bolton couldn't fix. No one could.

Again, she was getting way, way ahead of herself. She shut off her brain and forced herself to stay in the here and now, because right now, Ben was the answer to a whole lot of prayers. Josey couldn't do anything but sit in wonder at this man who had become such an important part of her life in such a short time.

Grandma had always talked about knowing she would marry Grandpa from the first time she saw him. It hadn't mattered that she'd been six and Grandpa had been ten or that their lives were so different. She'd just known. She'd always known.

Mom had been the same way. The way the story went, she'd come home from college on summer break and had seen the young grass dancer stomping in the middle of the ring. "I believe in love at first sight," she'd always said.

Josey watched as Ben sketched out the floor space that

the donated tools would need. She'd long thought Mom and Grandma had been over-romanticizing the past, glossing over the rough times and willfully choosing to remember only the highlights. She'd certainly never felt anything at first sight.

Until now.

She didn't know if this was love. How could she? She had no yardstick to measure it by. She'd never been in love, not really. Just that one time…but the way Matt had looked at her when she'd suggested they visit the rez had been enough for her to see that she'd been wrong.

Ben was different. Maybe she was different, too. That didn't make it love at first sight. But it made it something.

That night, Ben stood on the front step of the trailer and, holding her hands, kissed her. Knowing that Mom was on the other side of the door, listening, had Josey blushing a hot red. She hadn't felt like this since junior high.

"I had a nice time," she said in as low a whisper as she could pull off. "Mom loves you."

"Hmm," Ben hummed, kissing her again. "When can I see you again?"

"I have to pick up some books tomorrow. But I should be able to get back into the city by Tuesday night."

"Stay with me." The way he said it, so serious and yet so hopeful, made her melty. Suddenly, Tuesday was forever away.

"Yes."

"And Friday night? After practice?"

"School starts in two weeks." She had a to-do list that was nothing short of daunting. "Will you come to the school this weekend?"

His grin was wolfish as he ran his thumb over her lower lip. "Saturday—*after* we wake up. I'll have to leave by four

SARAH M. ANDERSON

to get to the gig in Sturgis, but we should be able to get the rafters up in the shop."

She managed not to exhale in relief. For so long, she'd struggled to walk in both worlds. And for way too long, it had felt like a solitary struggle, one that threatened to rip her into two distinct, unrecognizable parts. But right now, she felt almost whole.

So Ben couldn't guarantee her place in the tribe. So being with him was, in all likelihood, putting her place at risk. The fact that he was willing to work on it instead of bailing made it worth the effort.

"Sounds like a date."

He touched his lips to hers again as his fingers intertwined with hers. The connection wasn't sexual—heated, maybe. But there was more to it than just that.

Something *more*.

Josey wondered if it would be enough.

Eleven

"When's the new stuff going to be ready?"

This is what passed as conversation with Billy.

"Delivery on the lathe is scheduled for two months from now."

So far, so good, he wanted to add, but he kept that to himself. So far, he'd been able to keep the costs buried deep within the reports. So far, Dad was unaware of the huge expenditure. So far, this was going to work. But Ben forced himself to remain cautious. Until the equipment was here, where Ben and Billy could defend it—physically, if needed—there was still a lot of room for error.

"Damn." Billy was like a kid who couldn't believe Christmas was still months away. A few minutes later, he said, "When do I get to meet *her*?"

Ben stood back and looked at the frame. The bike was coming together. "Soon."

No way he could have her stop by the shop again, not after

the disaster that was the first time. But he might ask Billy to come over and play pool. That could work.

Lost in thought and focused on grinding the edges off the gas tank housing, Ben didn't hear the shop door open and shut. He didn't hear anything until someone clapped him on the back and said, "Ben! My man!"

Even over the sound of the angle grinder, he'd know that irritating voice anywhere. Bobby.

"Wild Bill! How's it hanging? Still to the left?"

Billy didn't even manage a grunt of acknowledgment. Ben kept his focus on the metal he was shaping. Over the preceding five weeks, the bike had taken shape at a satisfying pace. He stayed late on the nights Josey didn't come over, working side by side with Billy. Sometimes they talked; most of the time they didn't. It bordered on hanging out.

Blue wingtips—Ben blinked, but they stayed blue—walked in front of him. "Whatcha working on, bro?"

"What do you think? It's a bike."

Bobby whistled. "Wow. Who is she?"

Billy made an unhelpful, if amused, snort.

"Isn't anyone going to ask me how I'm doing?"

Billy and Ben shared a look. Did little brothers ever stop being irritating?

"Fine," Ben said. "Robert, how are you?"

"Touchy, touchy. I'm awesome, thanks for asking. Just came from talking to Dad." He waggled a finger at Ben. "You've been a bad little boy, Benjamin."

Ben's stomach sank. Bobby was usually a pain in the ass, but the irritating grin was more menacing than usual. "Get your finger out of my face. What are you talking about?"

"I've got big news from New York."

"Brother," Billy muttered, and Ben had to agree. Whatever was coming would either be bad or irritating. More than likely, both.

"Hear me out." Bobby's voice took on a serious tone. "I've been working on a synergistic deal that is going to grow our business across all markets, and I know you guys are going to love it."

Damn it. Josey had absorbed Ben's every free moment for the past month and a half. He'd actually managed to put Bobby and deals with producers out of his mind. Ben turned off his angle grinder and set it down. Hitting a man with an angle grinder was bad. Punching him was still on the table.

"You mean, like the jackets that no one buys and furniture that no one sits on? We're still carrying that loan."

"Or the time you promised those yahoos I'd build them all those crappy bikes in two weeks? And they sued me for breach of contract?" Billy's arms dropped. Ben made damn sure not to be in the way.

"Guys, guys! Come on—hear me out. This is totally different. A real game-changer." He glanced over Ben's shoulders as heavy footsteps echoed down the stairs and smiled that smile that meant nothing but trouble. "Besides, Dad just signed the contracts, so there's nothing you can do about it."

"You rat bastard," Billy growled, lunging.

On the one hand, Ben hoped Billy would pound the little zit into oblivion. On the other hand, he wanted to do the pounding himself.

"Knock it off," Dad roared as Bobby easily danced around Billy's big swings. "When the hell are you three going to grow up?"

"They haven't even let me explain what the deal is, Dad."

"Dammit, you kids," he said, sounding older than Ben remembered. He didn't "talk" to Dad often. Usually, he just mediated the shouting. "I ain't afraid to set you down the hard way, so sit down and shut up."

Ben and Billy glanced at each other. They could probably take both Dad and Bobby, but then the police would get involved and Cass would yell at them all for trashing the shop—again. Reluctantly, they backed down.

"That's more like it. A little family meeting." Dad let the blatant falsehood of that statement hang for a second before he pulled up a stool. "Bobby here has a hell of an idea. It's going to mean a lot more exposure, a lot more business—a lot more money. It's going to make Crazy Horse Choppers *the* name in custom bikes."

"How much?" Because, as far as Ben was concerned, that was the only question. What would this cost the company—and would they be able to survive the losses?

"What's the deal?" Ever the practical one, that Billy.

"I'm thinking big-time, guys." Bobby managed to look conniving and childishly excited at the same time. Man, Ben hated that look. "I signed a deal with a production company to do a series of webisodes."

"What?" Ben and Billy asked together.

Bobby had the nerve to look smug. "Webisodes. You know, episodes for the web? This is the first step. We build our platform, bring a dedicated viewership to the table and—" He spread his hands wide. "Boom. Reality show. This is a game-changer, guys. Big-time. This takes us from a boutique brand to an international player."

Ben shook his head. His ears must still be ringing from the angle grinder. Sounded like the little twerp had said...

"Did you say *reality* show?" Billy sounded truly surprised.

"We have to start with the webisodes." When Ben and Billy kept right on staring, Bobby elaborated. "I had a meeting with David Caine, head of FreeFall TV, and he loved the idea of a show that could compete with—and beat—*American Chopper.* We've got it all—gruff father, creative genius, bottom-line boss and me." He spread his arms wide, like he was welcoming his adoring public. "The total package. Caine loved the personality mix. Said it would lead to the kind of explosive family drama that both men and women aged eighteen to forty-five are flocking to."

"We're going to be on TV?" Was it possible that Billy sounded scared?

"Just the web, for starters. If we can hit Caine's viewer targets, we get a slot on the schedule. Think of it, guys! Free-Fall reaches over a hundred million potential home viewers!" Bobby grinned like an idiot.

Ben was having a little trouble understanding this so-called deal. "You—what? You *sold* our family?"

"Not exactly." He flashed Ben his salesman smile. Ben hated that smile. "We'll be paying a local production company to shoot and edit the webisodes." He actually seemed pleased with this.

Ben turned to Billy. "Did you know about this? Did you agree to being filmed?"

"Hell, no." Billy took a big breath and stood up to his full six-six height. "I won't do it."

"Ditto." Ben stood with his brother.

What would Josey say—what would she think? They'd hit a nice rhythm. She slept at his place a few nights each week. They ate dinner, played pool, watched movies and had the kind of sex that men fought wars over. Her mom liked him. Her whole tribe liked him—well, that might be a little strong, but at the very least, they didn't go out of their way to make his life more difficult, unlike his actual family. If he were a reality star? That would all change. It might even go away.

And then he'd be alone. With his family. Again.

"This is going to make us a lot of money," Dad said. "We need to bring in a little more capital, and this is the way to do it."

"Selling our family for a reality show? Are you serious?

You'd rather have cameras follow us around for months rather than let me *invest?*"

Whatever control Ben had was starting to slip. He knew his father didn't respect him. He could live with that—he had lived with it all this time. But to have the old man go so far out of his way to publically illustrate how little he valued Ben's skills?

He couldn't imagine that being hit with an angle grinder hurt any worse.

"I trust Bobby." His father pulled himself up to his full height and slapped his youngest son on the back. "Your mother would have been proud of you, son."

But Dad didn't trust Ben.

How pointless it had all been, Ben saw now, to spend years trying to earn his father's approval, his respect. To be someone his father could be proud of in a bar on a Friday night. Ben might as well have tried to make the sky yellow and the grass orange. He would have had more luck.

Everyone turned to look at him in a moment of calm before the hurricane-force storm. His whole life, he'd been the peacemaker who kept the wheels from falling off. He always kept his damned promises. That was who he was.

Wasn't it?

Maybe not. He didn't want to spend the rest of his life being the sucker with a spare tire chained to him, fixing a family that was always going to be broken. He wanted something different. Something more.

When he didn't rush in to talk everyone down and smooth ruffled feathers, Bobby did what he always did—he opened his big, fat mouth. "Then it's settled. We're going to need to conserve our resources to make sure we can pay the production company, so I canceled that big equipment order you guys put in."

Ben shot to his feet as he and Billy hollered, "You did *what?*"

Old habits died hard, and he found himself halfheartedly holding Billy back.

So this was what it came down to. In trying to keep one promise, he'd managed to break a whole bunch of his promises. The fact of the matter was that he'd never be able to keep his promise to his mother. He could keep trying until he was blue in the face, but there was no fixing his family. And his mother was dead.

He'd promised Josey, too. So much more than equipment. He'd promised that she would come first. Not just in bed, he realized, but in his life. Maybe he hadn't said the words out loud, but he'd promised her with his actions. And that was a promise he planned to keep.

"That's *my* equipment." Billy all but growled the response, momentarily lifting Ben's hopes. He wasn't alone in this. It was him and Billy against Dad and Bobby. He'd take those odds.

Dad snorted in unmasked scorn as he looked at Ben and said, "I didn't approve any of that new junk."

He didn't entirely trust himself not to tell the old man where he could stick his money, so he kept his mouth shut.

"Besides, we don't need any fancy new computer equipment," Dad snarled, turning his attention to Billy. "The old stuff works just fine."

"The old stuff is just that—old."

That was another nice thing about Billy. He didn't get bogged down in emotions like disappointment or failure. He worked best with anger. And there was no mistaking the situation—Billy was borderline violent.

"We can't afford that kind of equipment! I ain't paying for it!"

"We could afford it if you'd let Ben do his job and manage the company's funds."

It was nice of Billy to come to his defense, but Ben could take care of himself. There was still a chance he could talk his way out of this without getting his order canceled. He had to keep calm. "We're going to get a big tax write-off for donating this old stuff. We're going to get some good press—something I thought *you'd* understand," he said with a jerk of his chin toward Bobby. "And equipment that actually works would help production. We wouldn't lose time to recalibrating the tools."

"Or is that too much for you to get?" Billy added.

"You watch your tone." The old man's voice was low—too low. Too dangerous. A brawl was imminent.

"My tone?" Billy spat on the ground. "Let me tell you something. I've had it with you, old man. With both of you." Billy cracked his knuckles, just like Dad did. Like they all did. "All you do," he yelled, jabbing a finger toward Bobby, "is spend money you've done nothing to earn." Billy started in on Dad again, and Ben thought he saw the old man shrink back, just a little. "And you? You break things. You cuss at my guys. You bitch and moan like a little girl about how things used to be. You scare the customers. When are you going to get it through your dented skull that this isn't your business anymore? It's mine—mine and Ben's. We *work* here. You two are only here out of the kindness of our hearts."

"The kindness of *your* hearts?" The man seemed to puff up two sizes. "I built this business from the ground up. We are a family. This is a family business. You don't like how I do business?" He looked at Ben without attempting to hide his disappointment. "Well, you can just pack your things and go. And if you aren't a part of the business, then you aren't part of the family."

And there it was. The ultimatum. Maybe it had been years in the making, but it still hurt more than the last time he'd crashed his bike. Ben could either toe the family line, or he could go on his merry little way. He didn't need Crazy Horse—he had more than enough in savings to retire, and if he wanted to work, he'd have no problem finding another job. If the brawl was bad enough, Billy might walk anyway, and he and Ben could start a new business. Their own business, run it the way they wanted.

But if he wasn't a part of this business, he wasn't a part of the family.

He'd spent too many years doing everything in his power to keep the family together. If he quit, he'd be walking away from more than just a job. He'd be walking away from his *life*. He wanted to think that his mother would have understood that he'd tried his best—more than anyone else, she'd understood him.

More than anyone else until Josey came along, that was.

He *could* quit. Sometimes, a man had to cut his losses and walk away. He'd still have Josey. They could make a new family, a new life together. She could make him happy—happier than his father ever could.

Josey would understand about the equipment, he thought. Family was family, after all. She'd worked so hard to provide for her family, her tribe—that was one of the things he admired about her. She'd made a promise to her grandfather, and she'd kept it. He would not break his promises to her just to keep Dad and Billy from brawling. He would not be the kind of man to turn his back on her for such an everyday event.

What had she given up for him? He couldn't forget how all those kids *hadn't* looked at him that first day at the school—how he was practically invisible. He hadn't missed how people cut a wider berth around her mother at the powwow. He knew, deep down, that she had taken a risk being with him. She'd found a way to honor her promises *and* be with him.

Ben's family had always been the most important thing to him. Until he'd met Josey.

He wouldn't turn his back on her, on the sacrifices she'd made for him, especially not for a sixteen-year-old promise he'd never been able to keep. His mother wouldn't have wanted him to push away the one woman who made him happy.

No. Josey had put her reputation on the line for him. He owed her the same. That's what people did when they loved each other.

Josey walked in two worlds—she'd said so herself. Suddenly, Ben didn't so much understand what that meant as he felt it, deep in his heart. She might have been talking about the white and Lakota worlds, but that's what he needed to do, too—walk with his family *and* with her.

So this was him, looking for a new path to walk. There was more than one way to get that equipment, after all. It might take a little longer—he'd have to move a lot of his own money out of investments, but… He made a snap decision and held up his hands.

Amazingly, it worked. Everyone stopped yelling. All three of them turned to look at him. For a guy who rarely seemed to have the right answer, Ben was aware that they all expected him to fix this. Even Dad.

"Let me see if I've got everything straight."

The way the three other Boltons nodded—all heads moving at exactly the same tempo, at exactly the same angle—told Ben he had their undivided attention. Finally, he thought, after all these years. They were going to listen to him.

"Bobby wants to put us in a reality show. Billy wants expensive new equipment. I want to donate the old stuff to a school for a tax deduction. Dad, you don't want to pay for any of it."

"Damn straight I'm not going to pay for stuff we don't need," Dad grumbled.

Ben took a deep breath. He'd dreamed of this, but it hadn't gone this way in his head. "And if we're not in the business, we're not in the family."

"Damn straight," Dad muttered again, but this time, Ben saw the fear in his eyes.

I'm sorry, Mom. I tried, but I can't fix them. I can only fix myself.

"Then I quit. Effective immediately."

"You can't quit!" The way the three of them shouted it in unison made it ricochet around his head.

"I can, and I am. I met someone who showed me that there's more to life than keeping this business in the black," he said, pointing that particular remark at Dad. "I know who I am and what I want—and it's sure as hell not this daily war. For God's sake, do you know how hard I worked to keep my promise to Mom, to keep the family together? And for what? So Bobby can sell us to the highest bidder? So Dad and Billy can keep on killing each other over—what? Motorcycles? No. I can't do it, and I'm not going to die trying. Mom would've wanted me to find a nice girl and settle down, and that's what I'm going to do. Without any of you."

He had a moment of lightness, of peace. He could almost pretend Mom was looking down on him from heaven, saying, "You did your best, sweetie. Now go get your girl."

But then he heard a noise from the front of the shop—the sound of the door shutting. He turned just in time to see what looked like Josey's figure running out through the door.

"Josey!" he shouted as he ran after her.

He was pretty sure that, despite his best efforts, Dad and Billy were now trading punches in addition to insults, but he officially stopped caring. All that mattered was Josey. He had to get her.

But she was too fast for him. By the time he burst out of the front doors of Crazy Horse Choppers, she was in her car. He caught a glimpse of her face, saw the sobs that tore through her body. Their eyes met through the windshield. "Wait," he said.

Maybe she heard him, maybe not. If she did, she wasn't in any mood to listen. She slammed her car into Reverse, squealed the tires as she cut the wheel and was gone in a cloud of dust.

What the hell had just happened? Ben stood there in dumb shock, trying to figure out how much she'd heard and where he'd gone wrong. The equipment order had been canceled, webisodes, he'd quit and then he'd picked her over his family. Whatever had her freaking out, he had to find her. He wasn't about to decide he wanted to spend the rest of his life with her just to watch her run out the door.

He was going to fight for her, by God.

Where would she go? Frantically, he tried to think. The ridge. He'd check her apartment first, but he was willing to bet she'd gone to the ridge in the middle of nowhere. Now he just had to remember how to find it.

He was so focused on getting to Josey that he didn't hear Bobby come up behind him until the little jerk grabbed his arm. "Ben—what the hell? Are you gonna tell me—"

Ben snapped. He threw everything he had into the swing. A bone in his hand snapped, but the sparking pain was worth it. With a muffled *whump,* Bobby spun and went down like a sack of rotten potatoes.

"You traitor," he spat out at Bobby's motionless form. "You're nothing like our mother."

Then he was on his bike, riding as fast as he could, hoping he hadn't lost the way.

* * *

Josey heard the rumble of the bike from some far away place. She ignored it. Instead, she focused harder and harder on the land that lay before her. Her eyes searched the familiar contours—the small hill off to the left, the line of cottonwood trees that crowded around the skinny stream in the middle and the withered and brown grass that never ended under the bleak late-fall sky.

Didn't matter how hard she looked. She didn't see anything.

"Josey?" This distant shout was accompanied by the sound of something large crashing through the underbrush. "Are you up there?"

No. She was nowhere, because that was where she belonged.

This was where Grandma had always come after she'd spent too long in the white world. This was the place to get right with the spirits. But the spirits didn't seem to be interested in getting right with her.

Ben had just disowned his family for her. He was willing to give up his heritage, his life—everything he'd worked for, everything he'd built—for *her*.

He'd told his family he wanted to settle down with her. She should have been thrilled, honored—*excited*. But the only thing she felt was dread. He was going to give up everything for her.

She couldn't do the same for him.

She loved him, of that she had no doubt. For the first time in her life, a man—a relationship—made her happy. When they were together in his apartment, she almost felt like what the rest of the world thought didn't matter anymore.

Almost.

She couldn't hide in his warehouse mansion for the rest of her life. She wouldn't be his kept woman, wife or not.

She couldn't give up her place in the tribe, not even for the man she loved. She'd fought for too long to earn the grudging acceptance of her people. And unlike Ben, she couldn't turn away from the ties of blood. She had tried to walk in his world once, and she'd failed spectacularly. She couldn't turn her back on her tribe a second time.

But even so, she had the sinking feeling that, long after the affair with Ben Bolton had faded, people would still look at her funny. She was the same nowhere girl she'd always been. She didn't fit in the white world. Not with a white man, anyway. And despite her best efforts in the past two years, she didn't have a place in the Lakota world, either. Or she wouldn't, after she explained to everyone that Ben was no longer the savior of their little school.

She knew how people around here would take it—as a betrayal. Hers. She'd tried to straddle the line, walk in both worlds, but it hadn't happened. Instead of fitting in, she'd just made extra-sure that she didn't fit anywhere.

She'd thought that by coming back to Grandma's place, she'd find herself. She'd always found herself here before.

But not this time.

The spirits weren't interested in whether or not she was right with them. And it was all her fault. She was the one who'd forgotten who she was. Try as she might, she couldn't remember who that person used to be.

"Josey?"

He was getting closer. Damn that man and his attention to detail. Of course he'd remember this place and how to get to it. She should have just driven east until she ran out of gas. Then he wouldn't have been able to find her. No one would have, not even the ghosts.

He was panting. He must have run up the draw. She couldn't bring herself to look at him, so she shut her eyes and hid her face against her knees.

"Josey, let me explain."

She didn't want to hear his explanations. It hurt to have to listen to him. How had she been so foolish as to think that falling in love with him, of all people, would be enough? It wasn't. She'd wanted more. Too darn bad she hadn't figured out what "more" actually meant. Too bad for both of them.

He should have known better than to fall in love with a woman who didn't exist.

He started talking in a hurried, pinched voice. "I know I promised you that equipment, and I'm sorry that the order got canceled. You know I'd never break my promise to you, Josey. I can't get that equipment right now. But I'll figure out a way…"

She didn't care about the equipment. She'd accomplished her main goal. The school had drills and scroll saws and God only knew what else. Don could teach shop. Kids like Jared and Seth and Livvy could learn how to work with their hands and build job skills. She supposed she should feel good about that. But nothing was working like it was supposed to right now. That's how wrong everything was. She'd done what she set out to do. But she hadn't. The school was ready, but she hadn't found her place yet. The disappointment left her hollow.

She heard him move, and then his voice came from in front of her. He sounded like he was crouching down. "I broke my hand on Bobby's face for telling Dad and canceling the order. I'd do it again, too. In a second."

Against her will, her eyelids opened enough that she could see the red, swollen hand he held out to her. The whole thing was twice the size it normally was. It looked like it hurt.

"Josey, listen to me, please. I want to make this right. I—I can't keep the family together. Not like my mom wanted me to." He sounded so sad she felt her heart breaking in a new, different way. "But I'd rather lose them than you," he went on. "I quit. I'll get a different job, someplace normal, somewhere where my family can't get to me. I'll move some money around, get the things for the shop. I'll do anything to make it up to you, just…" He took a deep breath, and his hands—one broken, one not—rested on her knees. "Just look at me. Please."

A man should not sound so serious, so shaky, Josey decided. It made something weak inside her want to tell him not to worry, to make him feel better. But she wasn't going to. She hadn't misheard him. He would walk away from his family for her. He knew who he was. He didn't need a family or a group of people to accept or reject him.

Not like she did.

"Don't do this to me, Josey. To us. I'm not some outsider. It's me, Ben." The shakiness was gone from his voice. He was getting mad at her. Good. That would make the end easier. "I love you, okay? I love you, and you're just going to let that die because of my screwed-up family?"

He loved her? The way he'd said it—okay?—made it sound like he was negotiating a business deal. He was making a concession against his better judgment. He did not give his love freely, he expected something in return. He expected her to stay.

No. She didn't belong with Ben because she couldn't give up her family for him.

Then, for the first time, it occurred to her that maybe she didn't belong here on the rez, either.

Maybe the problem wasn't the man or the tribe.

Maybe the problem lay with her.

As this thought took root, Josey realized it was the unvarnished truth.

Of course—why hadn't she seen it before? *She* was the problem, thinking that she could define herself by her relationship with the tribe or with Ben. No wonder she didn't know who she was. She'd been too busy trying to be everything to everyone else.

Ben moved, and she hurried to shut her eyes. She knew one look into those baby blues might crack the dam of her resolve, and one crack could be fatal.

She felt the tender touch of his lips against her forehead, then he whispered, "I know where you belong, Josey. I know who you are. I'll wait for you until you remember."

Then he was gone, stumbling back through the underbrush. Soon enough, the rumble of his motorcycle shook the air, and then there was silence.

Until she remembered who she was?

Who did *he* think she was?

Twelve

"You're really leaving?" Jenny stood in the doorway of Mom's trailer, blocking Josey's exit.

"For the hundredth time, yes. Here," Josey said, hefting a copier-paper box full of shoes at her, "carry this."

"Do you have to go tomorrow?" Jenny sounded more like a whiny kid than a full-grown woman. And she wasn't moving.

"For the hundred and first time, yes. I start the new job on Monday." Josey did a slow turn, gauging how much stuff she had left to pack. Two more boxes, and then the suitcases of clothing. Four more trips, maybe five?

Jenny glared at her. "I don't understand why you had to get a job in Texas. I don't understand why you're leaving. When Ricky dumped me—while I was pregnant, may I remind you—I didn't tuck tail and run."

"I'm not tucking and running."

"Like hell you're not. So he turned out to be a jerk. What

man isn't?" Jenny said this as if it were a fact of life. "It's not like you work for him or anything. He'll never set foot on the rez again—not if he knows what's good for him. You'll never see him again. You don't have to leave."

Sorrow threatened to overwhelm Josey. She'd had an almost identical conversation with Mom last night.

But Josey wasn't leaving Mom and Jenny. If anything, they'd be the only two reasons to stay. But neither of them could see how much of a pariah Josey had become in the days following The End of Ben. People had stopped looking at her—even people she'd counted as friends, people like Don.

She couldn't stay here and be an outsider trying to fit in, and she couldn't let Ben be the way she defined herself. "You'll like Texas. Lots of cowboys. You can bring Seth down on summer breaks and stuff."

"Why Texas? Why go at all?"

"Because that's where the job is. Dallas is a nice city." Texas was someplace that had no memories. She'd looked at New York, but she didn't want to bump into the ghost of her grandparents every time she turned a corner. She wanted a blank slate, where no one had ever heard of Josey White Plume or Ben Bolton.

She needed to forget him, just for a little bit, while she tried to figure out who she was going to be from now on. Texas was as good as place as any to start over. People wouldn't look at her and wonder. They might assume she was Hispanic, but that wouldn't mark her as different. She would blend. Which was almost the same thing as fitting in. Almost.

Not that Jenny understood that. The perma-scowl on her face made that much clear.

Josey tried to appease her. "Hey—it's the Children's Hospital. I'll still be helping kids. I thought you'd like that."

"But not *our* kids," she snapped. "Not us." With that, she

stomped outside and dropped the box on the ground next to Josey's car.

She didn't want to leave with Jenny mad at her—but she couldn't see a scenario where Jenny was happy to see her go. That was a nice feeling. At least someone would miss her.

Would Ben? Josey tried not to think about him, but again and again he popped up in her thoughts. She'd spent far too many long nights wondering if he would come for her, but she hadn't heard a peep out of a Bolton in the past four weeks.

It was better this way. She didn't belong here or there, so she was going somewhere new and become someone new.

She'd found a job and rented an apartment. She was leaving, and that was that. It was better this way—a clean break.

That's what she told herself, again and again. She liked to pretend it was working. Tomorrow morning, pretending would get a lot easier. She needed to be in a different state than Ben just so she'd have room to think.

Jenny was leaning against the car, glaring at her. "You're coming by the school before you leave tomorrow, right? You're going to say goodbye to the kids, right?"

"Right. Around nine." One final hurrah to the old Josey White Plume.

She knew she couldn't leave without saying goodbye. She'd just have to do it quick, before her emotions got the better of her. After that, she'd be able to spend the thirteen hours in the car figuring out how she was going to fit into her new life.

Jenny wiped her hand across her eyes. "Is there anything I can do to change your mind?"

Josey went to her sister-at-heart and wrapped her up in a huge hug. "I'll come visit, okay? I'll come back for the graduations and stuff."

Sniffling, Jenny pushed her away and headed back into

the trailer, where she grabbed another box. "Yeah, but it won't be the same."

That's what Josey was counting on.

The next morning, Josey did a final sweep of her studio apartment. Empty, the small room seemed bigger than she remembered it. She was breaking her lease, but the new job in Dallas would pay her enough to make up the difference. She grabbed the box of books and headed down.

Her whole life was packed into the back of her car. Most everything she had owned had found happy homes with other people on the rez. She wasn't even taking the coffeepot. Just her clothes, her computer and a few things her grandparents had left her.

She fiddled around with the boxes, making sure they wouldn't shift during the trip, but everything was loaded and locked. She'd put it off as long as possible. Time for her final trip out to the rez. Then she could be on her way to a new life. A new Josey—whoever that was.

The drive took longer, like her car was trying to keep her here as long as possible. She took in the sweeping grasslands, the goofy roadside signs for Wall Drug and the sight of pronghorns dancing in the distance for the last time. She'd promised Jenny she'd come back, but she wasn't sure she could say goodbye to this place again and again.

Should have left yesterday, she thought as she bit her lip to keep the tears from breaking free. She shouldn't have agreed to this farewell, to giving every one of those kids— her kids—a hug and the books she'd picked out for them before she left. Because that's what she was doing. Leaving them all behind.

Lord, she didn't know if she could do this. Was she really telling herself that she'd never see Livvy or Seth or

Jared again? Was she really going to miss watching Kaylie grow up?

Josey had to stop before the final turn and take a bunch of deep breaths to get herself under control. Maybe she'd feel different in a few months. Maybe the new woman she was going to become would be able to come back to the rez every so often without feeling like another part of her was dying. Maybe she'd be able to come back when the eighth-graders graduated in six months. She could do that, right?

Once she was under control, Josey kept going. The sooner she got this over with, the sooner...

That thought died as she rounded the last bend. A massive, dual-wheel pickup truck—gray—with a custom trailer attached to it was parked next to the school.

Ben was here. He'd come for her.

But that wasn't all. Over the school door hung a sheet painted with the words *We Love Josey* and decorated with all the kids' handprints. All the kids were standing in front of the school. Oh, no. Livvy was holding flowers.

The emotional turmoil that already had her rolling turned vicious on her in a second. In that brief moment, she debated bailing versus just throwing up. Would she ever be prepared for that man?

No. Not in this lifetime. Maybe not even in the next.

She didn't have a plan B, so she made the snap decision to stick with plan A. It was still a plan, after all. No matter what he said, she had a job in Dallas, and she was leaving. Today. If he wanted her, he should have gotten his butt in gear during any of the preceding four weeks to come get her. That was that. And the kids? They were too young to understand how hard it was for her.

She parked at a safe distance from the familiar truck. Why did he have the trailer today? Had he gotten some equipment? He'd said he'd figure out how to get some. It had been one of the last things he'd said to her.

The second her resolve started to flutter, she snapped back to attention. So he'd gotten ahold of some equipment. Good for the school. Great for the kids. That wasn't her concern anymore.

She got out of the car. She was not leaving until she had said goodbye to the kids. That was the plan, and she was sticking to it, Boltons and signs and flowers be darned.

"We love you, Josey!" The kids all shouted in unison as Livvy ran up and handed her the flowers.

"We don't want you to go," Livvy said, tears spilling down her cheeks.

Josey pulled the girl into a fierce hug. "Oh, hon." The ground she'd been standing on felt shaky.

She'd thought no one—except Mom and Jenny—wanted her to stay on this rez. Had she gotten it all wrong? Maybe it wasn't what the grown-ups thought that mattered. She'd made a difference to these kids, and they loved her for it. Being too white or not Lakota enough didn't even figure into it.

Blinking, she looked up and saw Ben Bolton filling the door frame. Oh, he looked good. He looked like he always did—dark jeans, button-down shirt cuffed at his forearms, black boots—but just the sight of him took her resolve and threatened to smash it to smithereens.

He saw her. She could tell. He said something to someone over his shoulder, and then those long legs were closing the distance between them faster than her heart was beating.

Behind him, Josey saw Mom and Jenny shooing all the kids back inside. Jenny called to Livvy, but before the girl went back in, she shot Josey a grin that said she was in on it. "He came back. I think he always will." Then she was gone, running into the school and shutting the door behind her.

Out of the mouths of babes.

Ben pulled up before he was touching her, but only just. His eyes seemed unbelievably blue today. In fact, she was having trouble believing this whole thing.

"You're here." One hand waved up, like he wanted to touch her face but thought better of it. His hand was splinted and wrapped in a beige bandage.

She swallowed. "I'm leaving."

"I heard. Dallas." He stared down at her with a fierce intensity. "Your mom said your job starts Monday."

"Yeah." She wanted to tell him he looked good, that she was glad to see him, that she still hadn't figured out who she was so he might as well stop waiting for her. But that wasn't part of her plan, so she kept the words to a minimum.

"I missed you."

She didn't know what to say to that. It was the sort of thing that was easy to say, but hard to prove. If he'd really missed her, he'd have come for her sooner. Right?

They looked at each other for an unbroken moment before someone cleared his throat behind Ben. He turned to acknowledge…his brother, Bobby? And behind him, Billy? She checked, but she didn't see their father. She supposed she should be thankful for that, but three Boltons was at least two too many.

"Ms. White Plume, hi. Remember me? Bobby Bolton?" He talked a little differently, like his jaw was stuck halfway open.

"Hello."

He held up his hands in surrender. "I just needed to apologize to you, you know, for the mix-up. I, uh…" He stopped and swallowed.

"Go on." Staring at his boots, Ben sounded like a father listening to a recalcitrant child repeat a practiced apology. He flexed his hand inside the brace.

"I didn't mean to get Ben's order canceled. I wasn't aware of the situation, and I made an ass of myself. It won't happen again." He gave Ben a look that said, "How was that?" Ben nodded and turned to Josey.

He was waiting for her. He always waited for her.

"Um, okay. Apology accepted. Thanks." Bobby managed a crooked smile that made him look relieved.

Then Billy stepped up. His beard was trimmed down to a goatee, and a huge, angry scar cut down one side of his face. She'd never gotten a really good look at the oldest Bolton—too much shouting was distracting—but she was pretty sure that scar was new. "We're sorry about our dad, too. He can come off as a huge—" Ben cleared his throat in warning. "Jerk. He can come off as a jerk, but his heart's in the right place. Most of the time."

"I, um, I understand." Not really, but she was pretty sure everyone would be happier if they could stop this whole apologize-for-everything parade.

They all stood there, more or less looking at their feet, for a pained second. Then Billy said, "Yup," and he and Bobby moved toward the trailer.

"What's going on?" Josey hissed to Ben.

A metallic thud shook the ground, making both of them jump. She spun around to see the Boltons opening up the trailer. Something told her they weren't about to unload woodworking tools.

The corner of his mouth curved up, and even though she was sticking to her plan, dang it, certain parts of her went melty.

"We wanted to come out and tell you in person that our equipment is on order." His smile deepened. "We should be able to donate our old equipment in six months."

Stunned was such an inadequate word. "How?"

"Everyone calmed down in the E.R., and we had a chance

to talk. Well, I had a chance to talk while Bobby got his jaw wired, and Billy and Dad got stitched up, and they worked on my hand. Bobby's got a production deal he's working on, and the long and the short of it is that Billy and I convinced Bobby that helping the school is good for business. We'll donate the equipment, build the bike and film the whole thing. It'll be great press for the company *and* the school." Josey's jaw dropped, but Ben just gave her that almost-grin. "And Dad can't argue with all three of us. Not when we work together." He leaned forward. "And what's good for business is good for the family."

He'd decided this a month ago—and *this* was the first she was hearing of it? "But—but you quit your family and I'm leaving. Today. Now."

Ben stepped in closer—so close she could feel the heat radiating from his chest. "My father apologized to me. Wish you could have seen it," he added, his almost-smile deepening. "Never thought I'd see the day when he told me he was proud of me, but it happened."

Part of her was happy for him, because she knew how much that meant to him. But the other part? "It's been a month."

The flash of anger surprised her. Now that she thought about it, she wanted to throttle him. He'd done all of this—bikes and equipment and filming—without even bothering to pick up the phone?

No, she was *not* going to get melty or fluttery or anything just because he had the nerve to give her that private smile when she was mad at him.

"You weren't at your apartment the nights I came by, and I didn't think coming out to the rez unannounced was in my best long-term interest."

He'd come for her. He'd waited for her. Josey shook herself. She was sticking with the plan. She was *leaving.* "You could have called."

"I wanted to talk to you face-to-face. I wanted you to look me in the eye again." She could see the truth of that in his expression. He wouldn't have been able to change her mind on the phone, but when faced with the full-blown intensity of his gaze…she was wavering, and no amount of sticking with the plan was enough to keep her steady. "And after a few weeks of missing you here and there, I decided to wait until I was finished."

"Finished with what?" Stupid wavering voice, betraying her weakness around him. She couldn't even remember the plan she was supposed to be sticking to.

"I wanted to give you something." He put his hands on her shoulders and spun her around before she could say anything—not that she knew what to say, but still. He didn't let go of her, either. Instead, he pressed his front against her back. The unexpected contact sent an unwilling shiver through her body. Ben's scent—leather and the wind— surrounded her. He'd waited for her. He'd come for her. And he'd brought her…

Bobby was dusting the seat of a motorcycle while Billy crouched down behind it, rubbing a cloth over the chrome tailpipes. The bike had the same clean lines that Ben's did, but it was smaller, with a body that was a cheerful shade of red.

"A bike?"

"Your bike."

"Mine?"

His hands circled her waist, holding her tight. "Yes. I wanted to give you something to remember me by. Because I'll never forget you. I'll never forget who you are."

"Who am I?" She had to know what he thought. She couldn't leave without knowing who she was to him.

He took a deep breath, his chest rising against her back. "You're a complicated, conflicted woman, intelligent and beautiful. You cherish the past while working for a better future. You walk in both worlds, and you love them both. You expect better of me, and you make me better because of it."

She opened her mouth to say something, but nothing came out. Not even a squeak.

A low hum issued from his chest. She knew that sound. It was the sound of satisfaction. "I can't make you stay, Josey, but I won't give up on you. I'll come visit you in Texas, or New York—whatever it takes. No matter where you go or who you try to become, I'll still love you. Leaving won't stop that."

He loved her—the Lakota part, the white part, the messy way those two parts blended together. It was a simple fact that time and distance wouldn't change. He knew who she was, and he loved her anyway.

She might never truly be prepared for this man, but screw it. Winging it had its advantages, too.

She spun in his arms and kissed him. Oh, she'd missed his lips, missed being in his arms. But more than physical, more than sexual, she'd missed him. How could she have thought she could live without him?

He lifted her off her feet and swung her around. The hum got louder until suddenly he was laughing. "Stay," he said, resting his forehead against hers.

"I broke my lease. I don't have any place to live."

"Live with me. Stay with me." He kissed her again. This time, it packed more of a wallop, making her insides fluttery and melty at the same time. "I need you, Josey. Marry me."

"I need you, too." To pretend she didn't was foolishness embodied. If Ben walked beside her, willing to put one foot in each of her two worlds... She grinned. The journey was always easier with someone walking next to her.

A muffled cheer went up from inside the school. Josey broke away from Ben enough to see that, while no one had overheard their conversation, about thirty faces were pressed to the windows. Her cheeks got hot, only adding to the feelings running rampant. "We have an audience."

"Yeah." Billy's voice boomed across the grass. "You guys look like you can take it from here, so Bobby and I'll just be going."

Sweet Jesus, she'd forgotten about the other Boltons, too. Everyone had seen them kissing. Strangely, it didn't bother her as much as it used to. In fact, it felt just right.

"Always a pleasure, Ms. White Plume. Catch you later, Ben," Bobby shouted as Billy flipped up the trailer's door. The two of them hopped into the truck and took off.

Now some of the kids were banging on the glass, and Jenny's face appeared in the window of the door. "We've got to get out of here," Ben said. He took her hand and pulled her toward her car.

Except there wasn't room for both of them in there. She yanked him toward the bike. Mom could leave the school van here and take Josey's car home for the night. She and Ben could come back and get it tomorrow. "Your place. Take me to your place."

He pulled up short and kissed her again—a kiss full of promises, a kiss that delivered them.

"*Our* place. Come on, Josey. Let's go home."

* * * * *

See what's next for BILLY AND BOBBY
with the continuation of The Bolton Brothers
in September and November 2013!
Available only from Harlequin Desire

#2233 SUNSET SEDUCTION
The Slades of Sunset Ranch
Charlene Sands

When the chance to jump into bed with longtime crush Lucas Slade comes along, Audrey Thomas can't help but seize it. Now the tricky part is to wrangle her way into the rich rancher's *heart*.

#2234 AFFAIRS OF STATE
Daughters of Power: The Capital
Jennifer Lewis

Can Ariella Winthrop—revealed as the secret love child of the U.S. president—find love with a royal prince whose family disapproves of her illegitimacy?

#2235 HIS FOR THE TAKING
Rich, Rugged Ranchers
Ann Major

It's been six years since Maddie Gray left town in disgrace. But now she's back, and wealthy rancher John Coleman can't stay away from the lover who once betrayed him.

#2236 TAMING THE LONE WOLFF
The Men of Wolff Mountain
Janice Maynard

Security expert Larkin Wolff lives by a code, but when he's hired to protect an innocent heiress, he's tempted to break all his rules and become *personally* involved with his client....

#2237 HOLLYWOOD HOUSE CALL
Jules Bennett

When an accident forces receptionist Callie Matthews to move in with her boss, her relationship with the sexy doctor becomes much less about business and *very* much about pleasure....

#2238 THE FIANCÉE CHARADE
The Pearl House
Fiona Brand

Faced with losing custody of her daughter, Gemma O'Neill will do anything—even pretend to be engaged to the man who fathered her child.

REQUEST YOUR FREE BOOKS!
2 FREE NOVELS PLUS 2 FREE GIFTS!

(H) HARLEQUIN®

Desire

ALWAYS POWERFUL, PASSIONATE AND PROVOCATIVE

HDI3R

SUNSET SEDUCTION

The latest installment of USA TODAY *bestselling author*

Charlene Sands's miniseries

THE SLADES OF SUNSET RANCH

*All grown up, Audrey Faith Thomas seizes her chance to act
on a teenage crush. Now she must face the consequences....*

*U*sually not much unnerved Audrey Faith Thomas, except
for the time when her big brother was bucked off Old
Stormy at an Amarillo rodeo and broke his back.

Audrey shuddered at the memory and thanked the
Almighty that Casey was alive and well and bossy as ever.
But as she sat behind the wheel of her car, driving toward
her fate, the fear coursing through her veins had nothing to
do with her brother's disastrous five-second ride. This fear
was much different. It made her want to turn her Chevy
pickup truck around and go home to Reno and forget all
about showing up at Sunset Ranch unannounced.

To face Lucas Slade.

The man she'd seduced and then abandoned in the
middle of the night.

Audrey swallowed hard. She still couldn't believe what
she'd done.

Last month, after an argument and a three week standoff
with her brother, she'd ventured to his Lake Tahoe cabin to

make amends. He'd been right about the boyfriend she'd just dumped and she'd needed Casey's strong shoulder to cry on.

The last person she'd expected to find there was Luke Slade—the man she'd measured every other man against—sleeping in the guest room bed, *her bed*. Luke was the guy she'd crushed on during her teen years while traveling the rodeo circuit with Casey.

Seeing him had sent all rational thoughts flying out the window. This was her chance. She wouldn't let her prudish upbringing interfere with what she needed. When he rasped, "Come closer," in the darkened room, she'd taken that as an invitation to climb into bed with him, consequences be damned.

Well…she'd gotten a lot more than a shoulder to cry on, and it had been glorious.

Now she would finally come face-to-face with Luke. She'd confront him about the night they'd shared and confess her love for him, if it came down to that. She wondered what he thought about her abandoning him that night.

She would soon find out.

Find out what happens when Audrey and Luke reunite in

SUNSET SEDUCTION
by Charlene Sands.

Available June 2013 from Harlequin® Desire®
wherever books are sold!

HARLEQUIN® *Presents*

Revenge and seduction intertwine...

Andreas Xenakis has never forgiven or forgotten Siena DePiero. And when she becomes destitute after her family fortune disappears, he makes her an offer she can't afford to refuse: become his lover/mistress, for a price.

Andreas has waited years to get his revenge, but one night with beautiful Siena shatters his poor-little-rich-girl illusions and unleashes a passion that only a lifetime together might be able to sate... if he can convince her to stay.

FORGIVEN BUT NOT FORGOTTEN?

by *USA TODAY* bestselling author

Abby Green

**Available May 21, 2013
wherever books are sold!**

It all starts with a kiss

Check out the brand-new series

HARLEQUIN® KISS™

Fun, flirty and sensual romances.
ON SALE JANUARY 22!

HARLEQUIN®

A *Romance* FOR EVERY MOOD™

**Stay up-to-date on all your
romance-reading news with the
Harlequin Shopping Guide,
featuring bestselling authors, exciting new
miniseries, books to watch and more!**

The newest issue will be delivered right to you
with our compliments! There are 4 each year.

Signing up is easy.

EMAIL

ShoppingGuide@Harlequin.ca

WRITE TO US

HARLEQUIN BOOKS
Attention: Customer Service Department
P.O. Box 9057, Buffalo, NY 14269-9057

OR PHONE

1-800-873-8635 in the United States
1-888-343-9777 in Canada

Please allow 4-6 weeks for delivery of the first issue by mail.